Daisy was in a [barcode] **she startled aw** **clamped over he**

Her muffled scream quickly fell silent when Harry's face hovered into focus above hers. He pressed a finger to his lips in the universal sign of shushing and didn't remove his hand until she nodded her understanding to remain quiet.

Something was wrong. Even in her nearsighted haze, she could see Harry was strapping on his gun again. She pulled the sheet around her and sat up as he handed her the brown glasses they'd left in the living room.

She slipped them on, hoping that bringing clarity to his grim expression would give her understanding. "What is it?" she whispered softly. She heard one of the dogs growling from the foot of the bed, and all the beautiful aftermath of making love and sleeping contentedly in his arms vanished in a clutch of fear. "Harry?"

He pushed her phone into her hands. "Call 9-1-1. There's someone outside."

That was when Daisy jumped at the *pop, pop, pop* of tiny explosions and shattering glass out on the back deck.

MILITARY GRADE MISTLETOE

USA TODAY Bestselling Author

JULIE MILLER

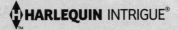

In honor of the seventy-fifth anniversary of Camp Pendleton,
home of the 1st Marine Battalion.

My dad and brother were both once stationed there.

For the real Muffy. Yes, that dog is a he. And yes,
he's in charge. Just ask him.

ISBN-13: 978-1-335-72139-6

Military Grade Mistletoe

Copyright © 2017 by Julie Miller

Recycling programs
for this product may
not exist in your area.

All rights reserved. Except for use in any review, the reproduction or
utilization of this work in whole or in part in any form by any electronic,
mechanical or other means, now known or hereinafter invented, including
xerography, photocopying and recording, or in any information storage
or retrieval system, is forbidden without the written permission of the
publisher, Harlequin Enterprises Limited, 225 Duncan Mill Road,
Don Mills, Ontario M3B 3K9, Canada.

This is a work of fiction. Names, characters, places and incidents are
either the product of the author's imagination or are used fictitiously,
and any resemblance to actual persons, living or dead, business
establishments, events or locales is entirely coincidental.

This edition published by arrangement with Harlequin Books S.A.

For questions and comments about the quality of this book,
please contact us at CustomerService@Harlequin.com.

® and TM are trademarks of Harlequin Enterprises Limited or its
corporate affiliates. Trademarks indicated with ® are registered in the
United States Patent and Trademark Office, the Canadian Intellectual
Property Office and in other countries.

Printed in U.S.A.

Julie Miller is an award-winning *USA TODAY* bestselling author of breathtaking romantic suspense—with a National Readers' Choice Award and a Daphne du Maurier Award, among other prizes. She has also earned an *RT Book Reviews* Career Achievement Award. For a complete list of her books, monthly newsletter and more, go to juliemiller.org.

Books by Julie Miller

Harlequin Intrigue

The Precinct

Beauty and the Badge
Takedown
KCPD Protector
Crossfire Christmas
Military Grade Mistletoe

The Precinct: Bachelors in Blue

APB: Baby
Kansas City Countdown
Necessary Action
Protection Detail

The Precinct: Cold Case

Kansas City Cover-Up
Kansas City Secrets
Kansas City Confessions

Visit the Author Profile page at Harlequin.com for more titles.

CAST OF CHARACTERS

Master Sergeant Harry Lockhart—He doesn't know how to be anything but a Marine. But after being gravely wounded and suffering from post-traumatic stress, this K-9 handler is sent home for the holidays to rethink his life outside the corps. He turns to his pen pal, whose sweet, angelic letters were a lifeline to sanity during his deployment and hospital stay. But this wounded warrior discovers he has one more mission—saving the only woman who can heal him.

Daisy Gunderson—She's dedicated to her students, her rescue dogs and Christmas. She isn't afraid of the taciturn, scarred Marine who shows up on her doorstep one winter's evening. But she's deathly afraid of the sick-minded stalker who's making her holidays a nightmare. Turning to Harry for protection makes sense. But giving this beast of a man her heart might be a fatal mistake.

Angelo and Albert Logan—Students of Daisy's.

Eddie Bosch—A science teacher at Central Prep Academy.

Bernie Riley—The school's PE teacher and basketball coach.

Stella Riley—The coach's wife is the jealous type.

Jeremiah Finch—Daisy's next-door neighbor helps keep an eye on the place.

Hope (Lockhart) Taylor—Harry's sister is worried about his mental recovery.

Pike Taylor—Hope's husband is a K-9 cop with KCPD.

Patch—The deaf Jack Russell terrier mix obeys hand signals and follows his nose.

Muffy—The gray-and-white shih tzu is the resident noisemaker.

Caliban—The aging Belgian Malinois and KCPD veteran lost a leg to cancer, but still has the heart of a warrior.

Prologue

"You're not the first marine this has happened to."

But it was the first time it had happened to *him*. Master Sergeant Harry Lockhart didn't fail. When he was given a mission, he got the job done. No matter what it cost him. But this? All the doctors, all the physical training and rehab, all the therapy—hell, he'd talked about things nobody knew about him, and it had gutted him worse than that last firefight that had sent him stateside in the first place—and they were still going to give him the boot?

Harry didn't know who he was going to be if he couldn't be part of the Corps, anymore.

His given name was Henry Lockhart Jr., but nobody called him by his daddy's name unless he or she outranked him or wanted a fist in his face. Henry Sr. was serving time in a prison in Jefferson City, Missouri for a variety of crimes, the worst of which was being a lousy excuse for a father. Between Henry's drinking, neglect and natural affinity for violence, it was a miracle Harry and his older sister, Hope, had survived to adulthood. Hope wouldn't have done that, even, if at the ripe old age of nine, Harry hadn't picked up his daddy's gun and shot one of the dogs that had attacked her when she tried to leave the house to get him food so he wouldn't starve.

A muscle ticked beside his right eye as a different memory tried to assert itself. But, with a mental fist, he shoved that particular nightmare into the tar pit of buried images from all the wars he'd fought, determined to keep it there.

"How many years have you been in the Corps?" The doctor was talking again.

If Dr. Biro hadn't also been a lieutenant colonel, Harry might have blown him off. But Biro was not only in charge of his fitness assessments, he was a decent guy who didn't deserve his disrespect. Harry met his superior's gaze across the office desk. "Seventeen, sir."

Biro nodded. "A career man."

"Yes, sir."

Hope was the only family he'd ever had, the only person he'd ever trusted, until he'd enlisted in the United States Marine Corps the day after he'd graduated from high school. The Corps had whipped his rebellious butt into shape, given him a home with regular meals on most days, introduced him to the best friends he had in the world and given him a reason to wake up every day and live his life.

Now his sister was married and had her own family. So he'd really, really like to keep the one he'd found. His physical wounds from that last deployment had left their mark on his stiff, misshapen face, but the scars were a sign that those had healed. He knew it was the mental wounds the lieutenant colonel was worried about.

Not for the first time in his life, Harry was going to have to prove himself worthy. He was going to have to earn someone else's unshakable trust in him again.

He was going to have to relearn how to trust himself.

Do this. That was Harry's motto. He couldn't lose the only home he had left. He scrubbed his fingers over the bristly cut of his regulation short hair. "You said I was improving."

"You are."

The medical brass seemed to like it when he talked, so he tried again. "I've done everything you asked of me these past four months."

Biro grinned. "I wish all my patients were as dedicated to following my orders as you. Physically, you could handle light duty, maybe even a training assignment."

"But…? Tell me the truth, Doc." Was he washed out of the Corps or not?

The lieutenant colonel leaned back in his chair. He wasn't smiling now. "You need to get your head on straight or we can't use you."

"You're not comfortable sending me out in the field?"

"I'd be doing you a disservice if I did." Biro leaned forward again, propping the elbows of his crisply pressed lab coat on the desktop. "At the risk of

oversimplifying everything you've gone through—
something broke inside you. I believe it's healing,
but the scar is still new and I don't want you to rip
it open again."

"I appreciate the honest answer." Harry did some
mental calculations on how long he'd have to play
this game before he could come in for his next as-
sessment and change the doctor's prognosis. "So,
peace and quiet, huh? Normalcy?"

The lieutenant colonel didn't understand how far
away from *normal* civilian life was for Harry. The
jarheads he served with didn't care where he'd come
from or how rough his altered face looked, as long as
he did his job. But on the outside, expectations were
different, and he was ill-equipped to handle them.

"That's my prescription."

"And I don't need pills on the outside? I just need
a shrink?"

Lt. Col. Biro opened a folder and pulled a pen
from his chest pocket. "That's my recommenda-
tion. If you can't sleep, or the mood swings become unbearable, call me. Otherwise, take the time
off. Relax. Give yourself a few weeks to reconnect
with civilian life. Enjoy the holidays. Get yourself
a Christmas tree and eat too many sweets. Kiss a
pretty girl and watch football all New Year's Day.
Whatever you like to do to celebrate." *Relax* and
celebrate sounded like daunting tasks for a man who
didn't have much experience with the examples on
the good doctor's list. "If you still want to after that,
make an appointment with my office in January and

we'll reevaluate your fitness to serve. Or, if you decide the clean break is what you need, I'll have your honorable medical discharge waiting for you. It's not like you haven't earned it."

Harry stood, clasping his utility cover, the Corps' term for a canvas uniform hat, between his hands. "I'll be back, sir."

The lieutenant colonel nodded before signing off on his medical leave papers and dismissing him. "You're from Kansas City, Missouri, right?" Harry nodded. "You might have snow there this time of year."

What was Biro going to prescribe now? Building a snowman to get in touch with the inner child Harry had never had the chance to be? "Sir?"

"My best buddy from basic training was from KC. I've always enjoyed my visits. I'll have my aide give you some recommendations for therapists you can see there."

"Thank you, sir."

Harry's cover fit snugly over his head as he pulled the bill down and hiked outside into the sunny Southern California weather. He drove to the base housing he shared with two other Non-commissioned Officers, or NCOs, slammed the door on his truck and hurried inside before he cussed up a blue streak that would have all of Camp Pendleton talking by sundown.

Thankfully, his bunk mates were both on duty so he had the house to himself. But that empty echo of the door closing behind him was a curse as much as it was a blessing. Damn, he missed the way his best friend used to greet him.

The remembered thunder of deadly fireworks and images of blood and destruction seared him from the inside out, leaving him with beads of sweat on his forehead and his hands clutched into fists.

Hell. The doc was right. His head wasn't on straight.

Using some of the calming techniques Lt. Col. Biro had taught him, Harry breathed in deeply through his nose and out through his mouth. Then he grabbed the pull-up bar hanging in his bedroom doorway and did ten quick reps until he felt the burn in his biceps, triceps and shoulders, and the anger that had flared behind his eyes receded.

He took the pull-up bar off the door frame and tossed it onto the bed beside the duffel bag he'd already packed that morning, having known he was either shipping out or going home by the time the medical team was done with him today.

You need to get your head on straight or we can't use you.

The lieutenant colonel's blunt words made the tiny, impersonal bedroom swim around him. Squeezing his eyes shut against the dizzying, unsettled feeling he hadn't felt since he was a little boy wondering if he was going to eat that day, Harry sank onto the edge of the mattress. He needed to find that happy place inside him. He needed to feel the holidays and the hope they inspired. He needed to find a way to push aside the nightmares and the anger and learn how to cope again. Or else the brass wouldn't let him be a marine anymore.

On instinct, he opened his duffel bag and pulled out a bulky, crumpled manila envelope that held the lifeline to sanity that had gotten him through that last hellish deployment and the long days in the hospital and physical therapy which had followed. He brushed his fingers over the torn envelope flap before sliding his thumb underneath and peeking inside. Now here was a little bit of sunshine. He pulled out a home-made angel ornament that had been a gift to him last Christmas. Then he studied the stack of cards and letters that were battered and smudged from travel and rereading. Words from a compassionate oracle who understood him better than he knew himself. His stiff jaw relaxed with the tremor of a smile that couldn't quite form on his lips.

Harry hadn't been this uncertain since he was that starving little boy with a black eye and clothes that didn't fit. He didn't need a shrink. He needed the Corps. But he'd need a miracle to make that happen. He needed the angel from all these cards and letters to work her magic on him again.

None of them were recent, but that didn't matter. The effect on him was always the same. He opened the very first letter and started to read.

Dear MSgt. Lockhart...

Chapter One

Dear Daisy,
Merry Christmas from your Secret Santa.

Daisy Gunderson stared at the gift tag, dotted with sparkles of glitzy snow, in the top right drawer of her desk and wondered who hated her enough to wage this terror campaign against her. This should be the happiest time of year for her, with the holidays and her winter break from school coming soon. Either somebody thought this sick parade of presents left on her desk or in her mailbox in the faculty work room was a clever idea for a joke, or that person intentionally wanted to ruin Christmas for her.

Typically, she made a big deal of the holidays, as evidenced by the greenery and ornaments decorating her classroom, and the hand-carved menorah and colorful Kwanzaa mat she had on display that had been gifts from former students. But the red glass candy dish filled with rat poison, the decapitated elf ornament and the X-rated card that had nothing to do with holiday greetings hidden away in her drawer were disturbing signs that not everyone shared the same reverence for celebrating this time of year.

The gifts were an eerie reminder of the tragic mistake she'd made three years ago that had cost her so dearly. But Brock was locked up in a prison cell, and would be until her roots turned gray. Daisy had already called the prison to confirm Brock Jantzen hadn't escaped or been accidentally released. These gifts couldn't be his handiwork. Men in prison who'd tried to kill their ex-girlfriends didn't get to send them cards and presents, right?

Daisy inhaled and let the long exhale flutter her lips. Of course not. These gifts had nothing to do with Brock. Or losing her father. Or even losing her mother, in a way. They had nothing to do with the scars on her chest and belly or her missing spleen.

Deciding that her thinking made it so, Daisy adjusted her purple-framed eyeglasses at her temples, spared a glance for the lone student muttering at the laptop on his desk, then looked up at the clock on the wall to wonder how much longer it was going to take Angelo to finish his essay before they could both go home for the day. Since she'd promised to give the teenager all the time he needed to complete his work, Daisy closed the drawer, picked up her pen and went back to grading papers.

But her thoughts drifted to the small stack of letters she'd locked away in a keepsake box under her bed at home. Letters from a marine overseas. Short, stilted and impersonal at first. Then longer, angrier, sadder. Master Sergeant Harry Lockhart yearned for quiet and routine just as much as he longed to complete the job he'd been sent to the Middle East to accomplish. She could tell he loved serving his country. That he loved the military dog he worked with, Tango. That he grieved the young men and native soldiers he'd trained and lost. She'd grieved right along with him when he'd written to say that Tango had been killed. Those letters had been part of a class writing project she'd initiated last year, with help from a friend at church, Hope Taylor, who had connected Daisy to her brother and his unit. She'd give anything to hear from Harry Lockhart again, even one of his short missives about the heat or the sand in his bunk. But sadly, those letters had stopped coming months ago. She hoped the unthinkable hadn't happened to her marine. More likely, he'd simply tired of the friendship after the class had ended and those students had stopped writing the servicemen and women with whom they'd been pen pals.

Now the only notes she received depicted graphic sexual acts and violence. All under the guise of a friendly game of Secret Santa.

She'd reported the gifts to her principal, and he'd made a general announcement about the appropriateness of everyone's anonymous gifts at the last staff meeting. And, she'd alerted the building police officer, who promised to keep an eye on her room and try to figure out when the gifts were being left for her. But, short of canceling the faculty party and gift exchange, and ruining everyone else's Christmas fun, there was little more she could do besides staying alert, and doing a little sleuthing of her own to try and figure out who was sending them. Daisy wondered if the wretched gifts might even be coming from someone who hadn't drawn her name in the annual gift swap—a disgruntled student, perhaps. Or maybe there was someone else in her life who thought this terror campaign was a cute way to squash her determination to make the most of every holiday celebration.

If that was the case, she refused to give in and take down one tiny piece of tinsel or play her Mannheim Steamroller music any less often. She already had enough reasons to mourn and resent the holidays. The Scrooges didn't get to win. If grief, abandonment and solitude couldn't keep her from saying *Merry Christmas* every chance she got, then a few morbid trinkets from a disturbed mind weren't going to make her say, *Bah, Humbug*, either.

"Finished. Five hundred and two words." A small laptop plunked down in front of her on her desk. "Before the deadline."

Daisy smiled up at Angelo Logan, a favorite student with as much talent as he had excuses for not doing his work. She knew no one in his immediate family had gone to college. And since that was a goal of his, she didn't mind putting in some extra time and pushing him a little harder than some of her other students. She skimmed the screen from the title, *The Angel and the Devil*, down to the word count at the bottom of the page. "Wow. Two words over the minimum required. Did you break a sweat?"

"You said to be concise." A grin appeared on his dark face.

"Did you map out why you're deserving of the scholarship?"

"Yeah. I talked about my home life, about being a twin and about what I can do for my community if I get a journalism degree."

Daisy arched a skeptical eyebrow. "In five hundred and two words?"

Angelo tucked the tails of his white shirt back beneath his navy blue sweater and returned to his desk to pull on his blue school jacket. "Can I have my phone back now, Ms. G?"

"May I?" she corrected automatically, and looked up to see him roll his deep brown eyes. The standard rule in her class was "No cell phones allowed," and anytime a student entered her room, he or she had to deposit their phones in the shoe bag hanging beside the door. Getting a phone back meant the student was free to go. Daisy smiled at the seventeen-year-old who looked so put upon by grinchy teachers who held him accountable for procrastinated essays and college application deadlines, when he probably just wanted to take off with his buddies for some Thursday night R & R. "You're too good a writer to miss this opportunity." She turned the laptop around. "Email me this draft and I'll get it edited tonight. I can go over any changes that need to be made with you tomorrow. Then we can send the whole thing off before Monday's deadline."

Angelo zipped back to her desk and attached the file to an email. "I've got basketball after school tomorrow. I won't be able to come in. Coach will bench me if I miss practice two days in a row."

Ah, yes. Coach Riley and the pressure he put on his players, despite the academic focus of Central Prep. "Can you do lunch?"

"Yes, ma'am."

She pointed to the shoe storage bag hanging by the door. "Grab your phone. Have a good night and I'll see you tomorrow."

But he didn't immediately leave. He exhaled a sigh before setting his backpack on the corner of her desk and digging inside. He pulled out a squished plastic bag with a red ribbon tied around the top and shyly dropped a gift of candy on her desk. "Thank you, Ms. G."

An instinctive alarm sent a shock of electricity through her veins. But then she saw the blush darkening Angelo's cheeks and realized she couldn't be paranoid about everything with a gift tag this time of year. Plus, the smushed present didn't look anything like the carefully prepared gifts she'd received from her Secret Santa. She feigned a smile before genuinely feeling it, and picked up the gift. "Are these your grandmother's homemade caramels?"

"Yeah. She wanted to thank you for the extra hours you're putting in on me."

Daisy untied the bow and pulled open the bag to sniff the creamy brown-sugary goodies. This present was safe. She'd seen it delivered, and there was nothing hinky about the candies wrapped in this modest bag. She could let herself enjoy it. "I love her caramels. She made a special batch without nuts for me?"

The blush faded as the grin returned. "I don't know why you want to eat them without the pecans, but she remembered that was the way you like them."

Daisy pulled out one of the individually wrapped caramels and untwisted the waxed paper. "Hey, between her and me, we're going to get you into college."

"Yes, ma'am. Um… I wanted to…"

Wondering how long Angelo was going to stand there before he said whatever was making him shift back and forth so nervously, Daisy popped the caramel in her mouth and started to fill the awkward silence. "These are the yummiest—"

She almost choked on the chewy treat when a sharp knock rapped on her door. "'Lo. You coming or what?" Although the baggy jeans and sideways ball cap were a vastly different look than the school uniform Angelo still wore, Albert Logan shared his twin brother's face. "Just because you got in trouble with the teacher doesn't mean I have to be late."

"I'm not in trouble," Angelo insisted.

"I don't care. I just know I have to drive your sorry ass home before I meet the guys."

"Granny's going to kill you if you skip dinner again."

"She ain't killed me yet." Albert jerked his head down the hallway toward the exit. "Move it."

"Hey, Albert." Daisy stood and offered a friendly greeting.

"Hey, Ms. G."

Despite looking alike, the two brothers couldn't be more different. "You know, my offer to stay after school and work with students who need extra help extends to you, too."

"I ain't in your class no more."

"You aren't anymore," she corrected. "I'm here with Angelo. I could easily tutor you, too. Get your grades back up so you can be on the basketball team again."

"Whatever." He turned down her repeated offer to help him raise his D's and F's into acceptable grades and pointed to his brother. "My car leaves in five. Be in it or walk home."

Although she was already plotting different arguments to convince Albert to get the help he needed, Daisy trained her smile on Angelo while he zipped his backpack and hurried to grab his phone. "Be sure to thank your grandmother for the caramels."

"Bye."

Once the teens had left her room, the silence of an empty school long after classes had ended closed in on her. Shaking off the instant sensation of loneliness before it could take hold of her, Daisy packed up her pink leather shoulder bag. She jotted a note to Bernie Riley, the boys' basketball coach, asking him to have a chat with his former player to encourage Albert to take her, or someone else, up on the tutoring offer. Without sports to keep him interested in school, she feared he'd wind up dropping out without a diploma. Then she grabbed her scarf and wrapped it around the neckline of her tunic sweater and pulled her coat from the closet before shutting off the lights and locking the door.

She'd make one quick stop at the faculty lounge to drop off the note, then head out. Besides hurrying home to let out her three dogs to do their business, she needed to get the place tidied up before showing the upstairs suite to the potential renter who'd answered her ad in the paper. Her friend Hope's husband was a KCPD cop, and he'd done a routine search on the guy and a couple of other tenant prospects to ensure they didn't have a criminal record or pose any obvious threat to her.

Having the dogs with her eased her concerns about living alone. But with the advent of the creepy cards and gifts, she'd decided that having a man on the premises, preferably an older one who reminded her of the security her father had once provided, would scare away whoever was threatening her. Besides, one of the hazards of living alone in the two-story 1920s Colonial her parents and grandparents had once lived in was that she was spending a small fortune renovating it. With taxes due at the end of the year and her savings already tapped out, thanks to the new HVAC system and roof she'd been forced to install, she could use the extra income of a tenant to get through the expense of the holidays.

Her steps slowed on the hallway tiles as her imagination surged ahead of her logic. Of course, the idea that her tenant might wind up being a serial killer, or even the sicko who was sending her that crap, was more than a little unsettling.

But no, Officer Pike Taylor had vetted this guy, so he couldn't be a danger to her. She sifted her fingers into the wavy layers of her hair and shook it off her shoulders. "Stop imagining the worst, Daisy Lou, and go home."

Her stop in the faculty lounge and work room revealed that she wasn't the only staff member working late this evening. "Hey, Eddie."

Daisy dropped her bag onto the chair beside one of the school's science teachers. It hit the seat with a thunk and Eddie Bosch laughed. "Taking a little work home tonight?"

"Just some papers to grade. And my laptop." Plus all the items a woman would keep in her purse, along with a few emergency snacks, a stash of dog treats and an extra pair of shoes in case the knee-high boots she wore got too wet with the snow outside and she needed to change before her feet froze. Daisy shook her head as her friend in the loose tie and pullover sweater grinned. "I guess I carry my life in there, don't I?"

"Well, you won't have to go to the gym and work

out if you keep lifting that thing." He closed the laptop he'd been working on and pointed a warning finger at her. "Now about that chiropractor bill you'll be getting..."

"Ha, ha." Squeezing his shoulder at the teasing remark, she circled around him and went to the wall of cubbies that served as the staff's mailboxes and searched the alphabetized labels for Bernie Riley's name.

She was glad Eddie had gotten to the point where he could joke with her. When they'd first started at Central Prep together, he'd had a sadness about him he wore like a shroud. He'd been new to Kansas City, had moved there for a fresh start after losing his fiancée to a long illness. Daisy had made it her personal mission to cheer him up and make him feel welcome. Now, he often made it feel like she was working with the teasing big brother she, as an only child, had never had.

But the comfortable camaraderie quickly ebbed as her gaze landed on her mailbox. She backed away when she saw the corner of a red envelope lying there.

Daisy startled at the hand that settled between her shoulder blades. "Don't worry." Eddie reached around her to pull the red envelope from her box and hold it out to her. "It's the teacher appreciation gift from the school board. A gift card to your favorite coffee shop. We all got one."

Taking the envelope, she clutched it to her chest, nodding her thanks. Eddie and a few other teachers were close enough friends that she'd shared some of the weird messages she'd been receiving. They'd all agreed that none of the staff could be responsible, and were now on the lookout for any signs of a disturbed student who might be sending the gifts. She appreciated that Eddie and the others were protective of her.

He pointed to other red envelopes still sitting in the mailboxes of teachers who'd already gone home, to confirm his explanation. "It's nice that they remember us each year. Although I'd trade gourmet coffee for a bump in salary if it'd do us any good."

Daisy agreed. "I hear ya."

He nodded toward the paper in her hand. "Is Riley giving you grief about keeping Angelo out of practice again?"

During basketball season, Bernie Riley gave everyone grief. "I think we've reached a mutual understanding."

"You mean, you've agreed to do things his way."

"Bernie and I both have the students' best interests at heart. He let Angelo stay with me today, and I'll adjust my schedule tomorrow." She held up her message about Angelo's brother. "Actually, I'm hoping he'll help me with Albert."

"Albert doesn't have half the brains Angelo does."

She was surprised to hear the insult. "Maybe we just haven't found the right way to motivate him yet."

"Uh-huh." Eddie pulled away and opened his satchel to stow his laptop. "Deliver your note and I'll walk you out." He nodded to the window overlooking the parking lot and the orange glow of the street lamps creating pockets of light in the murky evening air. "I hate how early the sun goes down this time of year."

Smile, Daisy Lou. Don't let anyone bring you down.

"Me, too." Daisy stuffed the note into Coach Riley's cubby and put on her insulated coat and gloves while Eddie pulled on a stocking cap and long wool coat. "Although, I do love it when the sky is clear at night, and the moon reflects off all the snow." She pulled the hood with its faux fur trim over her head. "In the daylight, the city snow looks dirty, but at night it's beautiful."

"You're a regular Pollyanna, aren't you," he accused with a smile, holding the door open for her. "It's twenty degrees, it's dark and I'm tired of shoveling my driveway."

"Scrooge."

"Nanook." He followed her out the door and walked her across the nearly empty lot to her car. "Are you expecting a blizzard I don't know about?"

She fished her keys out of her bag and unlocked the doors. "Fourteen degrees? That's plenty cold enough for me."

Eddie swiped his gloved hand across her windshield, clearing a swath through the blowing snow that had gathered there. "Want me to scrape this off for you?"

"You're a scholar and a gent, Mr. Bosch." Daisy thanked him for his gallant offer, but shooed him back to his own car. "The windshield wipers will take care of it. Go get warm. I'll see you in the morning."

"See ya. And hey, I didn't mean to sound flippant earlier. If there's anything I can do to help you with Albert, let me know."

"I will. Thanks." With a smile that no longer felt forced, Daisy climbed inside. Once she had her car started, he waved and trudged away to his own vehicle.

Daisy locked her doors and shivered behind the wheel, waiting for the wipers and defroster to clear her windows. Allowing the engine time to warm up, she crossed her arms and leaned back against the headrest, closing her eyes. She took on a lot this time of year, and she was tired. The stress of dealing with her Secret Santa, and the mental battle not to compare his gifts to the terror campaign Brock had waged against her three years ago, were taking their toll, as well. It was a challenge to get eight hours of uninterrupted sleep when every sound in the old house woke her. She made up for the fatigue by stealing short naps when she could. Like right now. Just a few minutes to rest before...

Daisy's eyes popped open as a sixth sense nudged her fully awake.

Someone was watching her.

She wiped the condensation off the inside of her window and peered out. Her gaze first went to Eddie's car. But he was busy brushing the thin layer of snow off the windows and top. His back was to her until he tossed the scraper into the back and climbed in behind the wheel. Then he was on his cell phone, chattering away in an animated conversation as he backed out of his parking space.

She pulled her glasses away from her nose to let the foggy lenses clear before sliding them back into place and scanning the rest of the staff parking lot. There were only four vehicles left. Coach Riley and the girls' basketball coach had both parked near the gym entrance while they finished with practice. She recognized the truck and van driven by the school custodians, as well.

The uneasy sensation of being watched crept beneath the layers she wore, making her shiver as if a cold finger was running along her spine. But a check of her rearview mirror revealed no one. Not one visible soul. Certainly no one spying on her.

Unless that person was hidden.

Behind one of the Dumpsters. Or around the corner of the building. Or peering out from the shadows of a dark room in the nearly empty school.

"Really?" Daisy smacked the steering wheel and pulled on her seat belt, irritated with the way her tired mind could play tricks on her. Those stupid gifts had spooked her more than she'd realized. "You are perfectly safe," she reminded herself, shifting the car into gear. Turning on her lights, she drove out of the parking lot. "The bad guys don't get to win." If she lived her life like a paranoid mouse, they *would* win. And she wasn't about to let that happen. She turned on a radio station playing Christmas music

24/7 and belted out rock anthems and traditional carols all the way home.

Daisy was a little hoarse from the songfest by the time she pulled into the detached garage behind her home. She pushed the remote button, closing the door behind her before unlocking her car and climbing out. Night had fallen, so she flipped the switch to turn on the Christmas lights lining the garage roof and fence, knowing they'd cast enough light to illuminate her path across the sidewalk to the deck and backyard entrance to her home. She smiled when she opened the door and looked out into the fenced-in yard. Beyond the edges of the walkway and deck she'd cleared, the red, green, orange, blue and white lights reflected off the snow like the warm glow of a sunset.

After pulling her hood up over her ears, she shut the door behind her and locked it. The damp bite of wintry air chapped her cheeks and hurried her steps past the gate and up onto the deck where the motion sensor light over the back door popped on, turning a small circle of night into day.

"Daisy? Is that you?"

Startled by the voice in the night, Daisy spun around. Once she'd identified the disembodied voice, she drifted beyond the edge of the light to bring her neighbor to the north into focus. "Good evening, Jeremiah." Although Jeremiah Finch's balding head was little more than a balloon-shaped shadow above the hedge on his side of the fence, she recognized his little Chihuahua in a pink and black sweater underneath the hedge where the snow wasn't as deep. As much as her neighbor loved his little princess, he liked to keep his yard in pristine condition, and would either immediately clean up after the dog, or hook her onto a leash and lead her to the bushes as he had tonight. "I see Suzy is bundled up against the cold. New sweater?"

"Knitted it myself. Are you coming down with a cold?" he asked, no doubt hearing the rasp in her voice.

"I'm fine. Just a little too much singing. And you?"

"I'm well. Suzy and I will be going in now. Good night."

"Good night." As formal and shallow as their conversations might be, Mr. Finch had proved himself to be a good neighbor. Besides maintaining a beautiful home, he didn't mind picking up her mail and watching over her house when she had to leave town. And she often returned the favor.

After he and Suzy had gone inside, Daisy slipped her key into the dead bolt lock.

One sharp, deep bark and the excited sound of yapping dogs told Daisy her furry family already knew she was home. She peeked through the sheers in the window beside the door and saw her beloved trio gathering in the mud room with tails wagging to welcome her before pushing open the door. "Yoohoo! Mama's home."

Muffy, her little tiger of a Shih Tzu led the charge out the door. A silver-and-white-haired boy cursed with a girl's name by the elderly owner who had to surrender him when she moved into a nursing facility, Muffy often made up for the insult by being the toughest and loudest guard dog he could be, if not the most ferocious-looking. Patch, her deaf Jack Russell terrier mix, took his cues from the other dogs, and followed right behind the smaller dog, no doubt barking because Muffy was. Both stopped for a friendly greeting and some petting before dashing out into the snowy yard. Patch, especially, loved being outside, leaping from snow bank to snow bank and snuzzling through the drifts as though feeling the cold against his skin made him giddy.

Her senior dog, Caliban, hobbled out the door on three legs. Daisy got the feeling that when her biggest dog stopped for a scratch around the ears, the Belgian Malinois was humoring her rather than seeking her affection. Poor guy. He'd spent a career at KCPD before the cancerous tumor that had led to the amputation of his left front leg forced him into retirement, and then he hadn't been able to live at his handler's home because the K-9 officer's child was allergic. Daisy reached inside the door to grab one of the rope toys that seemed to be the tan-and-black dog's only joy and tossed it out into the snow. As she watched him trot down the two steps into the yard, Daisy's heart squeezed in her chest. The experts who claimed that dogs didn't feel emotions didn't know Caliban. That dog was sad. He'd lost his job, lost his favorite person, lost his home and routine. When Pike Taylor had asked if she could take the dog for the last year or so he had left, Daisy had willingly opened up her home and her heart. Muffy and Patch had welcomed the older dog, although the two little spitfires made him cranky at times. Caliban had a good home here, but Daisy was still looking for the key to breaking through that reserve of his.

Smiling at the distinct personalities of each of her *children*, Daisy crossed to the railing to watch her three charges. Muffy was all business, inspecting the perimeter of the yard and trees along the back fence. Caliban was nosing around the gate and garage, avoiding the snow as much as possible. And Patch...

"Patch?" Daisy hiked her purse behind her hip and leaned over the railing. Where had he snuck off to? He wouldn't answer her summons unless he was looking right at her or following one of the other dogs. "Where did you go?"

Daisy looked down to see the clear impression of man-sized boot prints in the snow. The security light created shadows through the deck railings that had obscured them earlier. But there they were, a messy set of prints circling around the deck to the gas and water meters on the back of the house. She spotted Patch, his muzzle and jowls white with a snowy beard, following the tracks past the meters to the dormant lilac bushes at the corner of the house.

That wasn't right. Goose bumps pricked across Daisy's skin. She crossed to the side railing and squinted into the darkness beyond her porch light. Between the blowing snow and the shadows, she couldn't make out whether the tracks ended at the side of the house or if they continued into Mr. Finch's yard next door. Or maybe they'd originated from there? Maybe Jeremiah had spotted something that concerned him in the backyard. Still, she couldn't see the fastidious gentleman climbing over the chain-link fence when there was a perfectly good gate between the house and garage that granted easy access to the yard. It would be hard to tell exactly where the footprints led unless she went out in the knee-deep drifts to look with a flashlight. And as much as Daisy wanted answers, she wasn't keen on being anywhere alone in the dark.

She swallowed hard, trying to come up with a logical explanation as to why someone would be wandering around her backyard. She'd had the same utility worker from the city for years. He knew his way around her backyard, and didn't mind the dogs when they were out. Maybe he had a substitute walking his route, someone who didn't know there was only one gate. Patch spent a lot of time snuffling around in each footprint until he lifted his leg and peed in one. Why were there so many tracks? Had more than one person been in the backyard?

"Muffy? Caliban?" She put her chilled lips together and tried to whistle, but she doubted even a dog could hear the wimpy sound that came out.

Then she spotted Caliban's white muzzle as he carried his toy back up the steps to dutifully sit beside her. "Good boy." Had he sensed her fear? Did he just have impeccable timing? "Good, good boy."

Daisy scratched around his ears and rewarded him by pulling on one end of the rope and letting him enjoy a gentle game of tug of war. But the game ended quickly when Caliban released the toy and spun toward the back door. A split second later, Muffy zipped past her, barking like mad. That response could mean only one thing. They'd heard the doorbell at the front of the house. She had a visitor.

Although she was hardly prepped for company, she was more than ready to go inside. She caught Patch's attention and gave the signal for him to come. He dashed through the doorway in front of her.

The doorbell chimed again while she bolted the back door. The dogs raced ahead of her, yapping and tracking snow across the long, narrow rug and refinished oak of her hallway floor. Patch leaped over the two plastic tubs of Christmas ornaments she'd stacked beside the stairs, waiting for the tree she planned to get this weekend. Daisy hurried after them, dumping her purse on the bottom step of the staircase leading up to the second floor, pulling off her hood and stuffing her gloves into her pockets.

She pushed her way through the semi-circle of barking dogs, put Caliban and Patch into a sit and picked up Muffy, her brave boy who had the most trouble following orders and greeting an unfamiliar visitor. If this was the potential tenant Pike Taylor had okayed for her, she wanted time to explain that her pack of dogs were looking for treats and tummy rubs, not the opportunity to take a bite out of a stranger. Daisy flipped on the Christmas lights over the front porch and made sure the dead bolt was engaged before peering through the window beside the door.

"Wow." She mouthed the word, fogging up the glass.

The man standing on her front porch was hot, in a rugged sort of way. He stood six feet tall, give or take an inch. He wore a black stocking cap fitted tightly to his head and a beige coat that pulled at his broad shoulders and thick arms. With his hands down at the sides of his jeans and his legs braced apart, he stood there, unmoving. If it wasn't for the puffs of his warm breath clouding around his gray eyes, she'd have thought him a statue, impervious to the cold. Daisy's throat went dry at the inverse response of heat that could be nerves, or something decidedly more…aware…that he triggered inside her.

Not the fatherly figure she'd been hoping for. His face was a little too craggy to be handsome. The scars that peeked above the collar of his sweater and crept up his neck to the edge of his mouth and cheek to circle around most of his left eye, coupled with the stern set of his square jaw, added to his harsh look. She was certain Pike wouldn't send her anyone she wouldn't be safe with. Still, *safe* was a relative term. This guy didn't project calm reassurance so much as he looked as though he could scare off anyone who glanced crosswise at him. Although he would fulfill the purpose of having a tenant, she wasn't sure she'd be comfortable having a man like him in the house.

Still, if Pike said he was okay, she'd at least interview him.

She startled when his head suddenly tilted and his gaze shifted to her silhouette in the window. He'd caught her staring at him. He didn't smile, didn't wave an acknowledgement, didn't react, period. He simply locked his gaze onto hers until she muttered, "My bad," and hurried to atone for her rudeness. Muffy whined in her arms, and Daisy unbolted the door and opened it, leaving the steel-framed storm door secured between them.

The rush of heat she'd felt dissipated with the chill that seeped through the glass. "Hi. Are you here about the room to rent? I thought we weren't meeting until after dinner."

"Master Sergeant Harry Lockhart, ma'am," he announced in a deep, clipped voice. "Are you Daisy Gunderson?"

Recognition and relief chased away her trepidation and she smiled. "Master Serg…? Harry? Pen pal Harry?" She plopped Muffy down between the other dogs, then unlatched the storm door and pushed it wide open. "Harry Lockhart! I'm so excited to finally meet you." The dogs followed her out onto the brick porch and danced around their legs. Daisy threw her arms around Harry's neck, pressed her body against his rock-hard chest and hugged him tight. "Welcome home!"

Chapter Two

Welcome home?

Harry's vision blurred as something gray and furry darted between his legs. A mix of squeals and barks blended with the deafening boom and shouting voices inside his head, and his nose was suddenly filled with the stench of burnt earth and raw skin.

One moment, the memories were there, but in the next, he blanked them out and focused on the here and now. His body was hyper-aware of the softness wrapped around him like a blanket, and the creamy chill of the woman's cheek pressed against the side of his neck.

Daisy Gunderson was on her tiptoes hugging him. Bear-hugging him. Giving him a squeeze-the-stuffing-out-of-him kind of hug. What happened to polite introductions and handshakes? This wasn't the greeting he'd expected. She wasn't the woman he'd expected.

But when a woman hugged a man like that, it was his natural instinct to wrap his arms around her and...pat her back. He could hear his men ribbing him now, giving him grief over his lousy moves with the ladies the same way he gave them grief about staying sharp and keeping their heads down. He'd been short on this kind of contact for a long time. Months. Years, maybe. The instinctive part of him wanted to tighten his grip around her. A baser part of him wanted to reach down and see if the curves on the bottom half matched the ones flattened against him up top—or whether all that luscious body he felt was just the pillows of her coat squished between them. A different part of him, the part that was still fractured and healing, wanted to bury his nose in the sugar-cookies-and-vanilla scents radiating off her clothes and hair and skin, and let it fill up his head and drive out the nightmares.

Harry did none of those things. Although her scent was as sweet as he'd imagined, nothing else about this meeting was going according to plan. Dogs were barking. She was plastered against him. He patted her back again because he wasn't sure how he was supposed to react to this welcome. After all, he'd never met Daisy in person before.

She started talking before pulling away. "This feels like a reunion between old friends. I just got home myself. A few minutes earlier and you would have missed me. What are you doing here?" She shooed the dogs into the house and grabbed his wrist, pulling him in, as well. "Sorry. I'll stop talking. Come in out of the cold."

He watched the little gray-and-white fuzz mop dart back and forth across the area rug in the foyer while the white terrier jumped over him with a yip of excitement when he got too close. Those dogs were wired. They needed a good bit of exercise to take some of that energy out of them.

After locking the thick mahogany door behind her, Daisy pointed to the little one. "Muffy, down." Muffy? The long-haired one was clearly a dude, but he had to give the little guy credit for flopping down on his belly to pant until he got permission to go nuts again. "I can put them in their kennels if you want, but they'll mind if you tell them to stay down. Make sure Patch is making eye contact with you and use your hand. He's deaf. But smart as a whip. Jack Russells usually are. He knows several commands. Patch?"

She demonstrated a universal hand signal. The terrier sat, all right, but so did the Belgian Malinois. Who looked a lot like… That muscle ticked beneath Harry's right eye as he slammed the door on that memory and focused on the dog with the graying muzzle. Poor old guy had lost a leg. But those deep brown eyes were sharp and focused squarely on him, as if awaiting a command. Maybe the dog recognized another wounded warrior. "Is he a working dog?"

"KCPD-retired," she answered. "That's Caliban. He lost his leg to cancer. I inherited him when his handler couldn't keep him. Sorry about the mess. I'm in the middle of decorating for the holidays." Daisy was moving down the hallway beside the stairs, which were draped with fake greenery and red bows tied along the railing. She swerved around a couple of plastic tubs and kicked aside little bits of melting snow with her low-heeled boots. "Stick to the runner and it won't be slippery," she advised. "Could I get you something hot to drink? Coffee? Cocoa? Are you hungry? I baked a ton of cookies last weekend."

Did the woman never stop talking? He couldn't even say hello, much less ask a question or explain the reason he was here. "That's not necessary."

"Don't be ridiculous. It's cold. I'm cold. I'd be fixing it, anyway."

Clearly, she expected him to follow her through the house, so Harry pulled the watch cap off his head and stepped out. A parade of curious dogs followed him into a cozy kitchen that opened up to a dining room that appeared to be a storage area for unwanted furniture, more plastic tubs and paint cans.

"Ignore that room. My goal is to clear that out this weekend and finish decorating. I'm hosting my school's staff Christmas party next weekend." She shed her coat and scarf and tossed them over a ladder-back chair at an antique cherrywood table. "Have a seat."

"I wanted to talk about the letters."

"Sit." She pulled out a stool at the peninsula counter and patted the seat. "I'd love to talk about the letters you sent. Wish you'd kept writing after the school year ended." He'd stopped in June because that's when he... He hadn't written any letters from the hospital. "You're the first one of our pen pals I've met in person."

"That was nice of you to keep writing, even after

I dropped the ball." Harry put his leather gloves on the counter, unzipped his coat and settled onto the stool. He didn't have the heart to tell her that some of those pen pals were never coming home. "I want you to know how much my unit appreciated all the letters you and your class sent them. Even if we, if I, didn't always respond."

She was running water now, measuring coffee. "That was one of my more inspired projects. I started it with last year's composition class. Anything to get them to write. Plus, at Central Prep—the school where I teach—we encourage our students to be involved in the community, to be citizens of the world and aware of others. It seemed like a win-win for both of us, supporting the troops while improving their communication skills. When your sister mentioned your Marine Corps unit at church, looking for Christmas cards to send them last year, I jumped right on it." She tugged at the hem of her long purple tweed sweater after reaching into the refrigerator for some flavored creamer. As she moved about, Harry noticed that her glasses were purple, too, and so were the streaks of color in her chocolate brown hair. "I always model what I ask my students to do, so I adopted you. I don't mean adopt you like that— no one would adopt…you're a grown man. We drew names out of a hat. You were the one that was left, so you lucked out and became my pen pal. It's nice— no, amazing—to finally meet you in person." She stopped to take a breath and push a plate of sugar cookies decorated like Christmas trees and reindeer in front of him. "And now I'm rambling. Thank you for your service."

Now she was rambling? Harry was still replaying all the dialogue in his head to catch everything she'd said. "You're welcome. I was just doing my job. Thank you for your letters. They meant a lot to me."

"*You're* welcome. And I was just doing *my* job." She pulled two turquoise mugs from an upper cabinet while the earthy smell of coffee brewing filled the room. "You're home on leave for the holidays, I imagine. Are you visiting Hope?"

"I'm staying with my sister and her husband for a few days."

"How's their little boy? He's about two, right?"

"Gideon is…" A little afraid of the growly uncle who was rooming with him for the time being. Or maybe the fact that Harry was a little afraid of holding his energetic nephew without breaking him was what created the awkward tension between them. Who was he kidding? Pretty much every relationship was awkward for him right now. "Yeah, he's two in a couple of months."

"And Hope is pregnant with baby number two? That's good news. Although that apartment over her bridal shop only has two bedrooms, doesn't it? She and Pike will have to be looking for a bigger place soon." Daisy filled two mugs and carried them to the counter across from him. Although that bulky knit sweater covered the interesting bits between her neck and thighs, her leggings and boots hinted at earth-mother curves. He was busy filling in with his imagination the shape he couldn't see, enjoying the mental exercise a little more than he should when she set a fragrant, steaming mug in front of him, and cradled the other between her hands, warming her fingers. "What can I do for you, Master Sergeant?"

Harry dutifully pulled his gaze up to the blue eyes behind her glasses. "Top. You don't have to call me Master Sergeant every time. Top is the nickname for an NCO of my rank."

"All right, Top. What can I do for you?"

"I wanted to meet you in person and thank you for your letters."

"You said that already." She picked up a red-nosed reindeer cookie and dipped it into her coffee before taking a bite, waiting for him to continue.

Exactly how did a guy broach a subject like *I need the woman from those letters to help me regain my sanity? The golden, ethereal one with the soft voice, gentle touch and quiet mien I imagined in my dreams? I need that angel's healing touch.* He definitely didn't need a woman who talked nonstop, owned a pack of dogs and triggered a lustful curiosity he hadn't acknowledged for longer than he cared to admit. Harry picked up his mug by the handle, then turned it in his hands, staring down into the dark brew that reminded him of one of the colors of her hair. "Writing your students gave my unit something to do during the slow times. Getting those letters could really… You know, some days were harder than others, and, um…" This wasn't right. *She* wasn't right. Time to abort this crazy ass mission and call one of the shrinks Lt. Col. Biro had recommended for him. Harry set his mug down on the counter with enough force to slosh the coffee over the edge. "Sorry." He shook the hot liquid off his skin and shot abruptly to his feet. "Now's not a good time, is it?" While she retrieved a dish cloth to clean up his mess, he grabbed his gloves and headed toward the front door. "Sorry to show up on your doorstep unannounced."

"You haven't even touched your coffee." Harry strode past the trio of dogs who hopped to their feet to follow him. He heard Daisy's boots on the floor boards behind him. "You must have stopped by for some reason. We have lots to talk about, don't we? Your dog, Tango? Your friends who were wounded in that IED explosion? Are they okay? Were you hurt? I mean, I can see the scars, so clearly you were, but—"

"That was a different skirmish."

"You were hurt more than once?" Harry had his cap on, his coat zipped and the front door open when Daisy grabbed his arm with both hands and tugged him to a halt. "Wait."

Her fingers curled into the sleeve of his coat, tightening their hold on him. Harry glanced down at her white-knuckled grip, frowning at the unexpected urgency in her touch before angling around to face her.

"Please don't leave." Her face was tipped up, her eyes searching his as if she was struggling to come up with the right words to say. Odd. Words didn't seem to be a problem for her. "If you really have to go, I understand. And if you don't want to talk, that's okay. But…" She looked back over her shoulder, past the dogs and holiday decorations before she finally let go of his sleeve and shrugged. "Totally unrelated thing, but, before you go, would you do me a favor? I'm not saying you owe me anything. I mean, you barely know me—"

"I know you better than most people." Correction. He knew the person who'd been his lifeline to normalcy and home and hope. This chatterbox with the wild hair and effusive personality felt like someone different. "After reading your letters, that is. You shared a lot. About your ex, your parents, this house…" He glanced around at the refinished wood and fresh paint of the drafty old Colonial that was far too big for one person—even if she did live with a pack of dogs. "Some of your school stories made me laugh or made me want to wring someone's neck."

She took half a step back. "You remember all that?"

He'd memorized nearly every sentence. *Laughter. Concerns. Wisdom. Compassion.* The Daisy Gunderson he knew had shared her heart.

"I know the men and women I work with," he clarified. "My sister and her husband… I mean, you're not the only person I know."

He couldn't tell if the pinch at the corners of her mouth and eyes meant she was touched by his confession, or if she felt a little sad to learn how few connections he had outside the Marine Corps. "Thank you. I feel like I know you better than someone I just met a few minutes ago, too. You wrote some touching things that, well, some of them made me cry."

He made her cry? Harry shifted uncomfortably inside his coat. "Sorry about that."

"Don't be. You shared the truth about what was on your mind, what you were feeling. I was honored." She hugged her arms around her middle. "You made me smile sometimes, too."

So why wasn't he seeing that smile? The Daisy in his dreams always smiled. This was not going well. Daisy Gunderson was supposed to have a serene smile and a calm demeanor that made all the crap he had to deal with go away. But just because the real Daisy didn't fit the ethereal angel he'd imagined, it didn't mean he should blow her off. "You were going to ask me something?"

"Right." She shrugged one shoulder. Then she pointed at him, at herself, then back at him. "I'm here by myself and I wondered… Would you…?"

Now she couldn't come up with words? "Ma'am, I really should be going."

Her manic energy returned in a burst that faded into breathless hesitation. "One. Don't call me ma'am. My students call me ma'am, and it's after hours and I'm off duty. Besides, it makes me feel like I'm old enough to be your mother. And two… I could use a man right now." Now wasn't that a suggestive request. The parts of him south of his belt buckle stirred with interest, even as his chest squeezed with anxiety at the possibility she wanted something more than a pen pal, too. "But I don't have

a big brother or a boyfriend or a dad to call and..."
She gestured down the hallway toward the back of
the house. "Would you check something out for me?"

His disappointment surprised him more than the
relief he felt. "You've got a problem?"

"Maybe. I don't know." She tucked a stray lock of
hair back into the purple and brown waves behind
her ear. "I hope not, but..."

He could change a flat tire for her, or do some
heavy lifting or pull something down off a high shelf.
He owed the fantasy Daisy from his letters at least
that much. But as Harry waited for the details, he
read something more troubling than the awkward-
ness of this conversation in the blue eyes behind her
glasses. She was scared.

Seventeen years of military training put him on
instant alert.

"Show me."

Stopping only to put on her coat and order the
dogs to stay inside the mudroom, Daisy walked out
onto the back deck, and Harry followed. She went to
the railing and pointed down into the snow. "Those
footprints. Something seems off to me."

This was about something more than tracks
through her backyard. Her cheeks should be turning pink with the dampness chilling the air. Unless
the colored lights were playing tricks on him, her
skin had gone pale. The buoyant energy that had
overwhelmed him earlier had all but disappeared.
Seemed he wasn't the only one keeping secrets.

With a nod, he accepted the simple mission she

charged him with and went down into the yard. Stepping farther out into the snow so as not to disturb the suspicious tracks, Harry switched his phone into flashlight mode and made a quick reconnaissance. This was an awful lot of traffic through the yard of a woman who lived alone. And all of these tracks were too big to be Daisy's. His boots were digging into snow instead of sand, but the hackles at the back of Harry's neck went up just as they had overseas when he sensed an enemy lurking somewhere beyond his line of sight.

Trusting suspicions he wasn't sure he was equipped to deal with yet, he retraced his own path a second time, kneeling to inspect some of the deeper tracks. They'd frozen up inside after a bit of melting, meaning they'd been there long before the afternoon sun had reached them. He pushed to his feet and moved closer to the house to confirm that the deepest boot prints were facing the house, a good five feet beyond the gas and water meters. Harry looked up to a window with a shade drawn halfway down and curtains parted a slit to reveal the blackness of the room inside.

Harry glanced up at Daisy, who was watching his every move from the edge of the deck. She was hugging her arms around herself again. Something definitely had her spooked. "That's not just a case of a new meter reader guy thinking he could get out on that side of the yard, is it?"

"I don't think so. He'd only have to see that part of the fence once to know there's no gate over there."

And yet her visitor had walked back and forth multiple times, then stopped here to look inside that window. "What room is this?"

She paused long enough that he looked up at her again. "My bedroom."

Harry walked straight to the deck, braced one foot on the bottom planks and vaulted over the railing. The snow flinging off his boots hadn't settled before he'd turned her toward the door to walk her back inside. "You need to call the police. You've got a Peeping Tom."

Chapter Three

Harry sat in the darkness of his truck watching Daisy's light blue Colonial with the dark blue shutters and dozens of Christmas lights, wondering if she was going to give the balding guy at her front door the same kind of hug she'd given him when he'd left a half hour earlier. He already wasn't a fan of the older gentleman who'd insisted she leave the barking dogs on the other side of the glass storm door and finish their conversation on the brick porch where Daisy was shivering without her coat. If she hugged the guy, then Baldy was definitely going on Harry's do-not-like list.

Not that he'd handled either her enthusiastic greeting or grateful goodbye terribly well. But something simmered low inside him at the idea that Daisy's stuffing-squishing hugs were available to anyone who came to her front door.

Finally. The would-be renter handed Daisy a business card and shuffled down the steps. Harry exhaled a deep breath that fogged his window, relieved to see the thoughtless twit depart without a hug. He approved when Daisy crumpled the card in her fist, clearly dismissing the inconsiderate anti-dog man. She huddled against one of the big white pillars at either corner of her porch to watch the rejected tenant drive away.

"Go back inside," Harry whispered, urging the woman to show a little common sense and get out of the cold night air. But she was scanning up and down the street, searching for something or someone. Was she still worried about those snowy footprints in her backyard?

Harry hunkered down behind the wheel as her gaze swept past his truck. The brief glimpse of fear stamped in the big blue eyes behind those purple glasses when she'd asked for his help had been imprinted on his brain. And since the gray matter upstairs was already a bit of a jigsaw puzzle, he wasn't quite ready to have any worries about her safety lingering on his conscience. So he'd decided to hang out at least until Baldy left. But Daisy already had one pervert who thought looking through her bedroom window was a fun idea. She probably wouldn't be assured to know that he was still out here in the darkness, spying on her, too.

After one more scan, she went back into the house, petting the dogs and talking to them before closing the door. The colored Christmas lights winding around the pillars went out, followed by the bright light of the foyer. She must be moving toward the back of the house because a few seconds later, the lights decorating the garage went out, too. From this vantage point, Harry wouldn't know if she was fixing dinner or changing her clothes or making a path through the mess of projects in her dining room.

Not that it was any of his business how she spent her evenings. Baldy had left her house and it was time for him to go.

Harry started his truck and cranked up the heat, obliquely wondering why he'd felt compelled to sit there in silence, putting up with the cold in lieu of drawing any attention to his presence there. Probably a throwback to night patrols overseas, where stealth often meant the difference between avoiding detection and engaging in a fire fight with the enemy.

But he shouldn't be thinking like that. Not here in Kansas City. He watched Daisy's neighbor to the north open his garage and stroll out with a broom to sweep away the snow that had blown onto his front sidewalk. That was a little obsessive, considering the wind would probably blow the dusting of snow back across the walkways by morning. The neighbor waited for a moment at the end of his driveway, turning toward the same revving engine noise that drew Harry's attention. They both watched from their different vantage points as a car pulled away from the curb and made a skidding U-turn before zipping down the street. Probably a teenager with driving like that. The neighbor shook his head and started back to the garage, but paused as a couple walking in front of his house waved and they all stopped to chat. Yeah, Christmastime in suburbia was a real hotbed for terrorists.

Muttering a curse at his inability to acclimatize

to civilian life, Harry pulled out, following the probable teen driver to the stop sign at the corner before they turned in opposite directions. Although this was an older neighborhood, the homes had been well maintained. The sidewalks and driveways had been cleared. Traffic and pedestrians were the norm, not suspicious activity he needed to guard against.

Bouncing over the compacted ruts of snow in the side streets, Harry made his way toward his sister's loft apartment in downtown Kansas City, avoiding the dregs of rush hour traffic as much as possible. This evening's visit to Daisy's house needed to go on his list of dumb ideas he should have reconsidered before taking action. What had he thought was going to happen when he showed up on her doorstep? That the woman who'd sent him all those letters while he'd been overseas and in the hospital, would recognize him? They'd never exchanged pictures. He'd thought that trading news and revealing souls and making him laugh meant that they knew each other. That the same feeling he got when he saw her name at mail call would happen to him again when they met in person. If he was brutally honest, he'd half expected a golden halo to be glowing around her head.

Golden-halo Daisy was supposed to be his link to reality. Seeing her was supposed to ground him. The plan had been to let go of the nightmares he held in check, and suddenly all the scars inside him would heal. He could report back to Lt. Col. Biro and never look back after a dose of Daisy.

So much for foolish miracles.

Daisy Gunderson wasn't fragile. She wasn't golden-haired. And she certainly hadn't been glowing. She was a brunette—a curvy one, if his body's humming reaction to those impromptu bear hugs were any indication. A brunette with purple streaks in her hair and matching glasses on her nose and a need to chatter that just wouldn't quit.

And the dogs. He hadn't expected the dogs. Or the mess. Everything was loud and chaotic, not at all the peaceful sort of mecca he'd envisioned.

The fact that some pervert had been peeking in her bedroom window bothered him, too. He'd foolishly gone to a woman he only knew on paper—a stranger, despite the letters they'd shared—for help. Instead, it looked as if she was the hot mess who needed help.

Harry needed the woman in the letters to help him clear his head and lose the darkness that haunted him.

He didn't need Daisy Gunderson and her troubles.

He'd done his good deed for her. He'd assuaged his conscience. It was time to move on.

To what? What was a jarhead like him supposed to do for six weeks away from the Corps?

If he was overseas, he'd be doing a perimeter walk of the camp at this time of the evening, making sure his buddies were secure. Even if he was back at Camp Pendleton in Southern California, he'd be doing PT or reading up on the latest equipment regs or putting together a training exercise for the enlisted men he intended to work with again. He was used to having a routine. A sense of purpose. What was he supposed to do here in Kansas City besides twiddle his thumbs, visit a shrink and reassure his sister that she didn't need to walk on eggshells around him?

He supposed he could find the nearest mall and do some Christmas shopping for Hope, his brother-in-law, Pike, and nephew, Gideon. But even in the late evening there'd be crowds there. Too many people. Too much noise. Too many corners where the imagined enemy inside his head could hide.

Pausing at a stop light, Harry opened the glove compartment where he'd put the list of local therapists Lt. Col. Biro had recommended and read the names and phone numbers. Even before he'd finished reading, he was folding the paper back up and stuffing it inside beside the M9 Beretta service weapon he stored there. He closed the glove compartment with a resolute click and moved on with the flow of traffic.

He'd already made an appointment for tomorrow afternoon. He wasn't ready for an emergency call to one of them yet. Maybe he should ask his brother-in-law where he could find a local gym that wouldn't require a long-term commitment. He could lift some weights, run a few miles on a treadmill. That was all he needed, a physical outlet of some kind. A way to burn himself out until he was too tired to have any more thoughts inside his head.

It was almost eight o'clock when Harry pulled into the driveway beside Fairy Tale Bridal, the wedding planner business his sister owned. He pressed the buzzer and announced himself over the intercom before Hope released the lock and he jogged up the stairs to the apartment over the shop where she and Pike lived. He heard her warning Pike's K-9 partner, Hans, to stay before opening the condominium door. His sister had a quiet beauty that seemed to have blossomed with the confidence she'd found in marriage and motherhood. He was happy to see her soft smile when she welcomed him home.

But that smile disappeared beneath a frown of concern before she shooed the German shepherd into the living area of the open layout and locked the door behind her. "That coat is too small for you. You need to get a new one that fits."

"Guess I've filled out a bit since the last time I needed my winter coat. There's not much call for them in Southern California or the Middle East."

Although he'd fully intended to put his own things away, Hope took his coat from him as soon as he'd unzipped it. "You're later than I thought. Did you get any dinner? I can heat up some meatloaf and potatoes in the microwave." Seven months pregnant and wearing fuzzy house slippers with the dress she'd worn to work, she shuffled into the kitchen, hanging his coat over the back of one of the kitchen chairs. "Would you rather have a sandwich?"

Harry followed her, feeling guilty that, even after all these years, she felt so compelled to take care of him. "I'm good."

"Did you eat?" she stopped in front of the open refrigerator and turned to face him.

Hope was only a year older than Harry, and he

topped her in height, and had outweighed and out-muscled her for years. But she could still peer up at him over the rims of her glasses with those dove-gray eyes and see right into the heart of him, as though the tragic childhood they'd shared had linked them in some all-knowing, twin-like bond. Lying to Hope wasn't an option.

"No."

"I wish you'd take better care of yourself. It wasn't that long ago you were in a hospital fighting for your life. Besides getting winter clothes that fit, you need sleep and good food inside you." She nudged him into a chair, kissed his cheek and went to work put-ting together a meatloaf sandwich for him. "You found Daisy's house okay? What did you think of her?"

Harry pictured a set of deep blue eyes staring up at him above purple glasses, in an expression similar to the pointed look Hope had just given him. Only, he'd had a very different reaction to Daisy's silent request. Yes, he'd reacted to the fear he'd seen there and taken action like the marine he was trained to be, but there was something else, equally disconcert-ing, about the way Daisy had studied him in her near-sighted squint that he couldn't quite shake.

"She's a hugger." Surprised that those were the first words that came out of his mouth, Harry scrubbed his palm across the stubble itching the undamaged skin of his jaw.

But the faint air of dismay in his tone didn't faze Hope. In fact, something about his comment seemed to amuse her. "I told you she was friendly and out-going. She approached me that first morning in our adult Sunday School class. I'd still be sitting in the corner, just listening to the discussion if she hadn't sat down beside me and started a conversation."

Yep. The woman certainly had a talent for talking.

"There's Uncle Harry." Pike Taylor strolled into the living area, carrying their squirmy, wheaten-haired son, Gideon, who was decked out in a fuzzy blue outfit for bedtime. Even out of uniform, dressed in jeans and a flannel shirt, Pike carried himself with the wary alertness of the Kansas City cop he was. But the tall, lanky man who'd been there to protect his sister from both their abusive father and a serial rapist while Harry had been stationed over in the Heat Locker reminded Harry of an overgrown kid when he set his son down and chased him over to his play area in the living room. Even the dog got into the game, joining in with a loud bark and cir-cling around the toddler, which only made the little boy chortle with glee. That muscle ticked in Harry's cheek as the urge to smile warred with the images of something darker trying to surface. Gideon lost his balance and plopped onto the extra padding of his diaper before using the German shepherd's fur to pull himself back onto his pudgy little feet and change directions. "Look out," Pike warned from his wrestling position on the floor. "He's been ask-ing for his roommate all evening."

Gideon toddled over to Harry's knee, joyfully repeating a phrase that sounded a lot like "Yucky

Hair," which was apparently going to be his nick-name for the duration of this visit. Gideon's little fingers tugged at Harry's jeans and reached for him, demanding to be picked up. Although Harry was half afraid to hold the stout little tyke, he could feel the expectation radiating off Hope not to deny her son the innocent request. Unwilling to refuse his sister anything that would put a smile on her face, Harry picked up his nephew and set him on his lap. He pushed aside the salt and pepper shakers that Gideon immediately reached for, and let him tug at the buttons of his Henley sweater, instead. Hans lay down close by Harry's feet, keeping an eye on the little boy as if he didn't trust Harry with the toddler, either. Harry shifted in his seat, uncomfortable being the center of all this attention. Gideon batted at Harry's face and he lifted his chin, pulling away from the discomfiting contact. Hell, the dog was better with the child than he was. He needed to distract himself fast, or he was going to end up in a dark place that no one in this room wanted him to visit.

Turning his chair away from the watchful German shepherd, Harry latched onto the first thought that came to mind. "Daisy's a little scattered, isn't she?"

Pike tossed a couple of toys into Gideon's play-pen before rising to his feet and crossing to the table. "Scattered? You mean her house? She's been work-ing on it for three years. I can't imagine what it's costing her to redo it from top to bottom like that. Plus, she's doing a lot of the cosmetic work herself."

"I meant she rambled from one topic to the next. I had a hard time keeping up."

"She does live alone," Pike suggested. "Maybe she was lonesome and wanted to talk to somebody."

Hope snickered at her husband's idea. "She's been at school all day, with hundreds of students. She's had plenty of people to talk to."

"Teenagers," Pike countered. "It's not the same as talking to an adult."

Dismissing the explanation with a shake of her head, Hope opened a cabinet to pull out a bag of potato chips. "It's not exactly like you're Mr. Conversation, Harry. You're quiet like I am with new people. Maybe you made her nervous and she was chatting to fill the silence. I do that when my shy genes kick in."

Not in any universe would he describe Daisy Mega-Hugger as a shy woman. But maybe something about him *had* made her nervous. The scars that turned his ugly mug into an acquired taste? Not announcing his visit before showing up on her doorstep? Was there something more to those footprints in the snow than she'd let on? The idea of a Peeping Tom had upset her, yes, but now that he considered her reaction, she hadn't seemed surprised to discover signs of an intruder.

Hope ripped open the bag of chips and crunched one in her mouth before dumping some onto the plate beside his sandwich. "She is one of those women who seems to have a lot of irons in the fire. She's always volunteering for one thing or another. Daisy has the biggest heart in the world."

Harry pulled a toddler fist away from the tip of his nose. Was that big heart why she'd even considered giving Mr. Rude a place to live as her tenant? "I actually waited there a little while after I left. She had a guy coming in to talk about renting her upstairs."

Pike came up behind Hope and reached around her to snatch a chip and pop it into his mouth. "Mr. Friesen is the uncle of one of our receptionists at the precinct. I ran a background check on him for her."

"He showed up before I got out of there. I waited outside for half an hour to make sure he left without incident."

Hope's eyes were wide as she set the plate in front of Harry. "Without incident? That sounds ominous."

Harry ate a bite before breaking off a morsel of the soft bread for Gideon to chew on, in an effort to distract the toddler from grabbing the whole sandwich. "While I was there, she had me check out some suspicious tracks in her backyard. Looked to me like someone had been casing her house."

Pike pulled out the chair at the head of the table and sat. "Did you report it to KCPD?"

So, he thought the situation seemed troublesome, too. "I advised her to."

Hope moved a subtly protective hand to her swollen belly. "You checked out the house for her, didn't you? Her locks and everything are secure?

"She's got new windows on the ground floor. Dead bolts on the doors." But he hadn't checked any of them to see if they were locked. Surely, the woman had sense enough to... The second bite of his sandwich went stale in his mouth. He should have done that for her, at least.

Pike pulled Hope onto his lap, soothing her concern for their friend. "We've had a rash of burglaries across the city. Pretty standard for this time of year. Thieves looking for money or credit cards, or even wrapped presents they can pawn."

Either coveting his meal or sensing Harry's increasingly testy mood, Gideon squealed and stabbed at the plate, scattering the pile of chips across the table top. Harry shoved the plate aside and pulled the boy back, scooting the chair across the tile floor. His boot knocked against Hans, sending the dog to his feet with a startled woof.

All at once, the dark place inside his mind erupted with a fiery explosion. He felt the pain tearing through his flesh. He heard the shouts for help, the whimpers of pain.

Harry staggered to his feet. "*Platz*, Tango," he ordered, mixing the past and the present inside his head. "Hans, I mean. *Platz*." Pike's well-trained dog instantly obeyed the German command to lie down. Slamming the door on the flashback, Harry thrust Gideon into his frightened sister's arms and grabbed his coat. "I'm sorry. I need to walk around the block a couple of times. Clear my head."

"Harry?"

"Let him go, honey."

An hour later, Harry had come in from the cold, apologized to his sister, finished off the meal she'd saved for him and shut himself inside the bedroom he shared with Gideon.

The flashback had receded to the wasteland of buried images inside his head, although he was still having a hard time settling his thoughts enough to sleep. With Gideon snoring softly from his crib across the darkened room, Harry lay back on the double bed, using the flashlight from his duffel bag to read through the stack of cards and letters that normally soothed him on nights like this.

He grinned through Daisy's account of catching one of her students licking a potted plant in her classroom because the girl had been curious to find out what the sap oozing from the stalk tasted like. The girl had been perfectly fine, but the spate of dumb jokes that had followed would have given a stand-up comic plenty of material. The story had made his unit laugh to the extent that when any one of them made a boneheaded move, they'd teased the marine by calling him or her a plant-licker.

Gideon gurgled in his sleep, reminding Harry that he was the interloper here. In another couple of months, Hope and Pike would need this space for Gideon's new little brother or sister. Although he had every intention of returning to his duties with the Corps by that time, Harry acknowledged another stab of guilt. Maybe Hope wanted to redecorate this room. She had talked about expanding their loft into the shop's second-floor storage area, but a renovation of that scale wouldn't happen until after the baby's birth. Maybe he was in the way here, and Hope was too kind-hearted to say anything. Maybe he could camp out in their condo for just a few days longer, then find himself a quiet place to rent until his penance was over and he could report back to Lt. Col. Biro.

Daisy was looking for a tenant.

Harry returned the letter to the thick manila envelope. Nah. He couldn't. He needed a quiet place to heal for a month or so. He didn't want to get locked into a long-term lease, and he didn't want the place to be chaos central, either.

Dismissing the idea, he pulled another letter out of the envelope and turned his flashlight on it.

Dear MSgt. Lockhart,
I'm so sorry to hear about your friend. I know your work is important to you, but it sounds as though you need more time to grieve. Can you take leave for a couple of days? Please talk to someone there if you need to. A chaplain? Another friend? You're probably not comfortable dropping your guard like that.

When my father died so suddenly, I was in shock. It just didn't seem right that one tragedy should lead so soon to another one. That hurt me worse than Brock's assault because it felt so random. I could fight Brock, but I couldn't fight my dad's heart attack. Fortunately, I had a counselor who reminded me of the different stages of grief. That we all grieve differently, and that there's no timeline for when you stop being angry about your loss, or you get over feeling so heartsick. I sense that you're toughing this out. Be kind to yourself. I'm thinking kind thoughts for you.

Rainbows and unicorns and apple pie. Or chocolate cake? Steak dinner? What's your favorite food to eat or thing to do when you want to have fun and spoil yourself? Let me know, and that's what I'll imagine for you.

Despite her attempt at humor, Harry's thoughts darkened as he thought about Daisy's old boyfriend breaking into her apartment and attacking her with a knife. No wonder she was leery of someone scoping out her house. Harry swung his legs off the side of the bed and sat up. A few letters earlier, Daisy had said her ex had been sent to jail. How long would a guy be locked up for a crime like that? Was she worried about him returning? Sleep was feeling more elusive than ever as Harry made a mental note to ask Pike to check into her ex's status.

His breath stuttered through his chest as he forced his concerns for her aside. There were cops for worries like that. He wasn't in a good place to take on somebody else's trouble right now.

Harry turned his gaze and the beam of his flashlight down to the rest of Daisy's letter, needing to recapture the peace and comfort of her words.

If I was there right now, I'd listen to whatever you wanted to say. For however long it

*takes to get it all out. If the feelings are too pri-
vate for you to share with me, maybe you could
write them down just for yourself. Get them
out of your head so there's not so much you're
holding inside that you have to deal with. You
don't have to send the words to me, but I find
journaling like that helpful.*

*Believe it or not, I'm a good listener. And a
good hugger, or so I'm told. If you're ever in
Kansas City, I'll have a hug waiting for you.*

Take care,

Daisy

The hint of a smile eased the tension in him at the
hugging part. She hadn't been kidding. But the smile
never fully formed. Because Harry had taken her up
on that offer to write down all his anger and grief.
He'd sent her a vitriolic letter—three and a half pages
of crap that no one should have to know about. And
she'd still answered with another note saying that
she had cried on his behalf because she understood
that he'd never been able to, that marines didn't cry.

She'd helped him through that nightmare when
all had seemed lost. Forget about his own present
needs for a second. He owed Daisy a lot more than
a brusque brush-off and the silent blame he'd heaped
upon her for not living up to the image of the all-
knowing angel of his fantasies.

Steeling himself for a half-formed mission, Harry
folded up the letter and returned it to the others be-

fore shutting off the flashlight and tying his boots back onto his feet.

Hope was right. He was a man of duty. His brain might have a missing chunk filled with anger and darkness, but he was trained to protect and serve.

Maybe all Daisy needed was a man on the premises to scare off lusty lookie-loos or potential burglars or a crazy ex-boyfriend. She'd be safe. He wouldn't feel this added guilt. Hope wouldn't look at him with those big worried eyes and he'd have a roof over his head for the next six weeks.

Hard to argue with logic like that.

Peace of mind and sleep weren't happening tonight until he dealt with at least one of the problems bugging him.

He picked up his phone, but realized he didn't have a number for Daisy. Just the Gunderson address.

Harry grabbed his keys and his coat and quietly shut the bedroom door behind him. Pike and Hope were in the living room, snuggling on the couch as he suited up and walked to the front door. "I'm heading out for a bit."

Hope set aside the book she'd been reading. "It's late."

Harry pulled on his watch cap. "It's not that late."

She shifted her awkward weight and turned to face him. "Are you okay? Did I say something that upset you earlier?"

Pike had muted the news show he'd been watching and risen to his feet. The taller man was watching Harry very carefully, probably to make sure he didn't say or do anything to hurt her. Good. Harry was glad that Hope had someone in her life who loved her enough to take care of her like that.

Did Daisy?

I don't have a big brother or a boyfriend or a dad to call.

Harry leaned over the back of the couch to kiss Hope's cheek. "I'm fine. I just need to run an errand."

"Take the spare keys," Pike advised. He strode into the kitchen and pulled a ring of keys from the nearest drawer before tossing them across the room to Harry. "In case you're out after we've turned in. I'll put Hans in his kennel, Remember, the down command is—"

"*Platz.* Yeah, I know." He knew a lot about working with trained dogs like his brother-in-law's K-9 partner. That had been his job overseas. Him and Tango and... *Nah. Don't go there.* Shutting down the memory he couldn't yet face, Harry stuffed the keys into his pocket. "Hans won't be a problem."

"Let us know how Daisy is doing," Hope prompted.

No sense lying about where he was headed. His sister knew him better than he knew himself. Harry paused in the open doorway before letting himself out. "I will."

Chapter Four

Sleep wasn't happening tonight.

Although the logical part of Daisy's brain told her that the scratching noise at her bedroom window was the wind blowing bits of wintry debris against the panes, she sat up for the third time, clutching her spare pillow against her chest. She stared at the gingham drapes, her vision blurred by nearsightedness and shadows, half expecting them to fly open and reveal a man standing on the other side. Fighting to form a coherent thought over the pulse thundering in her ears at that unsettling idea, she picked up her old tortoise-shell framed glasses from the bedside table and blinked the glowing red numbers of her clock into focus.

2:49 a.m.

Her breath seeped out on a weary sigh. Her six o'clock alarm was going to beep mighty early if she couldn't shut down her fearful imagination and get some sleep.

She flipped on the lamp beside her, flooding the room with a gentle light. Muffy stretched his short legs on top of the quilt, scooting closer to reclaim the warmth from the crook of her knees where he'd been sleeping. Patch sat up behind her on the far side of the bed, his posture indicating he was alert and ready to start his day.

"Not yet, you silly boy," she chided. But her smile was the only invitation Patch needed to climb into her lap to lick her chin in exchange for some petting. Daisy indulged in a few seconds of warmth and affection before looking past him to see Caliban curled into a ball at the foot of the bed. The older dog seemed annoyed to be disturbed from his slumber yet again and tucked his nose under his front leg and tried to go back to sleep.

The furnace kicked on and Daisy startled again, rattling the headboard against the wall. Damn. Who needed some creeper sending her unwanted gifts when she could spook herself with her own imagination? By the time she reminded herself that the drapes were swaying because the vent beneath the window stirred the air and not because a Peeping Tom had moved them, all three dogs were sitting up, looking at her intently, no doubt wondering if they were going to be taking another jaunt with her around the house in search of an intruder they knew wasn't there.

A floorboard creaked overhead and Daisy tilted her gaze up to the ceiling. Again, logic said the noise was the old wood of the house shifting with the changing temperature of heat ducts running through the walls and beneath the floors. But the board above her creaked a second time, and a third, and logic became a voice her fears wouldn't let her hear anymore.

That sounded like footsteps. It shouldn't be possible. The dogs would be barking. The police had taken her statement about the tracks in the snow. She'd locked all her doors and windows.

Downstairs.

She hadn't been upstairs since she'd hung the lights and greenery on the bannister earlier in the week. Not that there were any outside doors or even fire escapes on the second floor where someone could…

Something banged against an upstairs wall and she jumped inside her skin. Brock had shattered the lock on her apartment door the night he'd broken in to assault her. The locks on this house were doubled, heavier.

Didn't make any difference.

She heard another bang. Then another that was slightly muffled.

"Sorry, guys." Daisy couldn't stay there a moment longer, fighting her imagination. Pushing the dogs aside, she tugged on her sticky-bottomed slipper socks and tied her chenille robe over her flannel pajamas. "If I don't double-check what that noise is, none of us will be getting any sleep."

While the dogs jumped down from the bed and stretched, Daisy crossed to the window. She pulled aside the edge of the drape and window shade underneath, bracing for a gruesome face staring at her from the other side. Relieved to see nothing but the dim glow of moonlight reflecting off the snow in her backyard, she exhaled the breath she'd been holding. Quickly tucking the window coverings back into place, she pulled her cell phone and keychain with its pepper spray from her purse and opened the bedroom door.

Daisy had no qualms about running up her utility bill if it meant feeling safe. She flipped on the hall light and the mudroom light, along with lights in the kitchen, dining room and living room. After a quick check of her office, she flipped the switch to illuminate the second-floor landing and climbed the stairs. Muffy followed at her heels, with Patch darting up ahead of them.

"Please be a tree branch caught in the wind and knocking against the side of the house. Or snow." Snow was good. Normal. Maybe a clump had melted off the eaves and landed on a window sill. Ignoring the logic against anything melting in this single digit weather, Daisy nodded, liking that explanation for the discomforting noises. "Please be snow."

A sweep of the empty landing allowed her a moment's reprieve to look back down to the foyer. Her heart squeezed in her chest when she saw Caliban standing with his one front paw on the bottom step, anxiously looking up at them. He bravely hopped up two more steps, but his paw slipped from underneath him on the polished wood and he reversed course, returning to the area rug at the foot of the stairs and sitting at attention. "It's okay, boy. You keep an eye on things down there."

Although she suspected he'd push through his phobia and obey the command to join them if she called to him, Daisy turned her back on Caliban's big brown eyes and flipped on the switch in the first bedroom. This was the room she planned to rent out, along with the bathroom across the hall. This was where she'd heard the floorboards creak, and the thump against the side of the house. Her eyes had barely adjusted to the bright light when Caliban let out a deep warning bark. Daisy answered with a startled yelp. A split second later, someone banged loudly at her front door and she clutched her chest at the double shock to her heart. "Brock is in prison," she reminded herself out loud. "He can't hurt you."

But Secret Santa could.

All three dogs ran to the door, sounding a ferocious alarm. Her thumb hovered over the numbers on her phone. 9… 1…

"Daisy! Daisy, open up!" Did she know that voice? A man's voice. Loud enough to be heard above the barking dogs. Brock had a scary, loud voice, usually slurred by alcohol. But this voice was sharp, succinct. "It's Harry Lockhart. Open up!"

"Harry? What…?" The relief surging through her veins made her light-headed as she raced down the stairs. She pocketed her phone and pepper spray before attacking the locks.

He was a broad, imposing silhouette outside her storm door until she thought to turn on the porch lights. Adding the glow of Christmas colors to his stern features did nothing to ease the frantic mix of urgency, confusion and relief that made her hands tremble on the latch. Her fingers lost their grip on the storm door as he pulled it right out of her hand.

"Caliban, *sitz*!" Harry ordered the dog to be quiet and sit while he clamped his hands around her shoulders and pushed her inside.

"Is that German? What are you doing here?" she asked, obliquely marveling that her Belgian Malinois obeyed commands in two languages, while Muffy managed to ignore orders in any language. "Is that a gun?"

She barely had time to recoil from the holster cinched around his thigh with a web belt before he trapped her between the thick wood door and his equally solid body and locked the dead bolt. The holster and webbing were military khaki in color, a sharp contrast against the dark denim of his jeans. The wood was cold against her back as he flattened her there, folding his shoulders around her as his chin swiveled from side to side, his gaze inspecting the crossroads of archways that met in the foyer.

"You turned on all the lights. What's wrong?" he demanded in the same clipped tone he'd used with the dogs. Without surrendering the shielding posture of what she could only describe as warrior mode, he pulled back just enough to look down into her eyes.

"What's *wrong*?" she echoed. Daisy curled her fingers into the nubby weave of his charcoal sweater exposed by the unzipped front of his coat, feeling so off-balance by his surprise visit she needed something to cling to. She wanted to push some space between them. The heat of his body was too close, his gun too hardpressed against her hip, his masculine scent too distracting for her to think straight. But all she could do right now was hold on. "Have you been watching my house?"

His gray eyes narrowed on her face. "Your glasses are different."

"What?" Oh, right. She was wearing the brown frames. That observation was as random as her own thoughts right now. Damn, the man had muscles. With his coat hanging open she could see that the burn and shrapnel scars on his face and neck ran down beneath the collar of his sweater. He had been so terribly hurt. An explosion? A fire? He'd nearly lost his eye. And that would be a shame because they were such a beautiful, deep color, like an endless, storm-tossed ocean. *Focus!* Daisy shook her head, still not comprehending why he was here. But she could answer his question. "I have different frames for different outfits. These are my knock-around-the-house pair."

He pulled away as suddenly as he'd pinned her there, and her knees nearly buckled as chilled air rushed between them. He peeled off his gloves and stuffed them into his pockets. "Caliban, *fuss.*"

Foos? Apparently, that meant *heel*, at least to Caliban. Harry spun away to inspect her living room, with the three dogs trotting behind him. Once she thought she could walk again, Daisy tightened her robe around her waist and followed them in a circle through the house, watching Harry stop at every window and door.

When they ended up back at the front door, Daisy caught the sleeve of his coat and halted his search. She could think now, at least clearly enough to know that she still didn't understand why Harry Lockhart was prowling through her house at three in the morning. "What are you doing here?"

"I didn't check your locks before I left earlier."

Was that supposed to make sense to her?

"Why did you turn on all the lights?" he went on. "Something's happened. I thought someone might have broken in."

He *was* spying on her. Daisy tucked her hair behind her ears, unsure whether to be flattered or creeped out. He couldn't know about those disturbing gifts she'd been receiving, could he? Why was this man who'd been so anxious to leave her the last time they'd met so eager to protect her now?

"Daisy?" he prompted. "Why did you turn on the lights?"

She responded to that succinct tone as readily as the dogs had. "I heard noises upstairs. Something hit the side of the house. We went to check."

And then he was off again, taking the stairs two at a time with Muffy and Patch right on his heels.

Daisy knelt on the rug beside Caliban, hugging her arm around his shoulders to stroke his chest, soothing the thrumming energy quaking through the muscular dog's body. Either she was absorbing his edgy alertness or she was just as anxious as Caliban to know what Harry was seeing up there before muttering the word "Clear" as he left each of the three bedrooms and bathroom.

She pushed to her feet as he turned off the second-floor lights and came back down the stairs. Patch's entire butt was wagging with excitement at the late-night adventure as he propped his front paws against Harry's thigh. But Harry pushed him away and signaled for the Jack Russell mix to sit. With Muffy dancing around his legs, paying no heed to either voice commands or hand signals, Harry muttered something under his breath and bent down, picking up the dog.

"Har…" For a split second, Daisy reached for the Shih Tzu, worried that Harry's limited patience couldn't tolerate another yap. Instead, he set Muffy down between Caliban and Patch, pushed the dog's rear end to the rug and ordered him to sit. He repeated the process twice more before Muffy got bored enough with the exercise that he stretched out on his tummy and batted at Harry's boot.

She arched an eyebrow in apology. "He's a hard-headed one to train."

"Yep. He needs an exercise program like fly-ball or agility training to get rid of some of that energy." Harry straightened, propping his hands at his waist, reminding her of the military issue gun strapped to his side before his chest expanded with a heavy sigh. "You got any irate neighbors?"

"What?"

"Kids who'd be out roamin' the neighborhood on a school night?"

"No." Not the questions she'd expect from a man who hadn't found anything to worry about. Daisy was suddenly aware of the icy remnants of slush left from Harry's boots on the foyer rug soaking through her socks and chilling her from the toes up. "What did you see?"

He pulled back the edges of his coat to splay his fingers at his waist. "The house is secure. No signs of forced entry."

"But?"

"It's hard to tell from inside, but it looks as though someone used the side of your house for target practice." He inclined his head toward the stairs. "You've got a snowball stuck in the screen of that bedroom window. I opened it up to knock it clear, but it looked like a couple more splats of snow just beside the window, too."

A few minutes ago, she'd been hoping that snow was the culprit. Not so much now. "Someone was throwing snowballs at my house at three in the morning?"

"Whoever threw them isn't there anymore."

"Or never was." She thought of the sick gifts hidden inside her desk at school and wondered if she was just being paranoid to think that that terror campaign had somehow followed her home. "Maybe the snow fell from the roof or blew off the branches of Mr. Finch's sweet gum tree."

"Don't discount your instincts. Being aware of danger is half the battle of protecting yourself from it."

But Daisy wasn't any kind of marine. "Sometimes my imagination gets the better of me. I remember that night Brock broke into my old place… I told you about him, didn't I?" She interpreted his unblinking glower as a yes. "I know he's locked up in Jefferson City…" She put up her hands, blocking the mental images of her ex's bared teeth and wild eyes, and that bloody knife poised above her. "Bad guys don't get to win." Brock didn't even deserve the time and space inside her head to sour her thoughts. "A few snowballs aren't any kind of threat. I let the noises of the old house get to me."

"The ghosts caught in our heads can be—"

"Relentless." His gray eyes locked on to hers, wide with surprise before narrowing to question her response. That look was too intense for her to hold, so she shrugged, nervously catching her hair behind her ears before looking directly at him again. "You said that in one of your letters."

"I remember. Didn't think you would." Harry shifted on his feet and glanced at the front door, as though an alarm had just gone off inside him, warning him it was time to end the conversation and leave. But then that piercing gaze was on her again. "One of the parts that made you cry?"

"I suppose I wear my emotions pretty close to the surface." While he barely showed his at all, other than this urgent need to escape her company. Again. "Crying isn't a bad thing." When he nudged aside the dogs and turned toward the door, Daisy followed, stopping him before he could leave. "Do I make you nervous, Harry? Is it the dogs? Do they remind you of Tango?"

"Tango?" He glanced over the jut of his shoulder at her.

"Your K-9 partner."

"I know who Tango is." A muscle ticked across his taut cheekbone and he reached for the doorknob. "Was."

"I'm so sorry you lost him. I can't imagine what that must feel—"

"Like I said, everything looks secure. I'll walk around the house to see if I can find signs of where the snowballs came from before I leave."

"You're leaving?"

Of course he was. Only the crazies wanted anything to do with her. Harry just had an overdeveloped sense of responsibility, the kind of alertness and protective instincts she'd expect from any career marine. He might be her friend on paper. She might have fancied herself half in love with the uniformed hero from their letters. But that was her fantasy, not his.

That still didn't stop her from moving between him and the door and sliding her arms beneath his coat, hugging him around the waist. With his coat unzipped, she could get closer than she had yesterday evening. Turning her cheek against the thick wool of his sweater, she felt his body warming hers. She breathed in the rugged smells of soap and Harry. "Thank you for looking out for me."

A fraction of a second longer and she would have pulled away. But his thick arms folded around her, his hands settling between her shoulder blades to gently pat her, almost as if he was trying to burp a baby. Not the most romantic embrace. But this was just a friendly hug, right? At least he wasn't holding himself completely stiff or pulling away. Maybe the taciturn tough guy with the scarred-up face was shy? Smiling against the beat of his heart at that tender notion, Daisy snuggled beneath his chin. She knew he wasn't married, and he'd never mentioned a girlfriend—past or present—in his letters. His sister, Hope, seemed to be the only woman in his life. Could his reticence to carry on a social conversation extend to the physical expression of emotion, as well? But if he was willing to hold on right now, she was more than willing to surround herself in his strength and heat.

"It's not like I could sleep, anyway." Harry's hands stopped their awkward petting and settled against the ribs of her chenille robe long enough for her to feel their warmth seeping through the layers of cotton and flannel. His voice was a growly whisper at the crown of her head. "Thought I'd put my time to good use. Those boot tracks worried me enough that I wished I'd run a security check like this before I left. Felt guilty that I hadn't. It was so late I didn't want to wake you. I thought it'd be enough to watch from outside the house."

"So I'm not the only one with insomnia. We're a

pair. I toss and turn in bed out of worry, and you sit out in the cold out of guilt."

His nose rubbed against her temple as he breathed in deeply. Was he sniffing her hair? Why not? Standing here, she'd been memorizing the scent of his clothes and skin. His fingers curled into the back of her robe, pulling it tight across her back for a moment, as if he wanted to hold on tighter but didn't dare, before he released her and backed away. Filled with static electricity, a few wisps of her hair clung to his sweater like tiny, grasping fingers. Before she could smooth them back into place, his hand was there, tucking the wayward strands behind her ear. "Will you be okay now?" he asked.

She reached up to cup the side of his face. When he tipped his head away from her touch, Daisy suspected it was vitally important that she not retreat. Maybe it wasn't just shyness, but a self-consciousness about the wounds he couldn't hide that made him so awkward around her. She brushed her fingertips along his cheek and jaw, noting the rough textures, marveling that she could still feel the warmth and rugged bone structure beneath the stiff ridges of scar tissue there. She imagined Harry had a lot of reasons why socializing and human contact might not come easily for him. "I know you went through something horrible when you were deployed. I'm sorry if bringing up Tango upset you. I know that dog meant a lot to you. You mentioned him in nearly every letter."

Harry turned away and opened the door. "I'll wait on the porch until I hear the dead bolt engage."

Clearly, they hadn't gotten off on the right foot in person. But if he wouldn't talk to her, she didn't know how to fix whatever the problem was between them. "I'm sorry if I've done anything to—"

He spun around, leaning toward her with such a hard expression that she backed away a step. "Don't apologize to me. Ever. If anything, I owe you." Owe her what? But he wasn't going to explain that cryptic remark, either. He was already on his way out the door. "Good night, Daisy."

"Good night, Harry."

She locked both doors and moved to the side window to watch him stride through the snow around the side of the house. A few minutes later, apparently satisfied with his reconnaissance mission, he returned to his truck and climbed inside. She was glad to see he had a cup of coffee waiting for him, and wondered if it was still hot. She wondered if he'd appreciate her brewing up a fresh pot and offering to refill his disposable cup. If sleep was an issue, though, he wouldn't want more caffeine. And if being with her made him so edgy, he'd probably appreciate her turning off the lights and going back to bed so he could relax his vigil. If she could do that much to thank him for both his service to their country and standing watch here on the home front, she would.

"Good night, Top," she murmured before shutting off the Christmas lights. "Come on, boys."

Daisy turned off the rest of the lights except for the lamp beside her bed. After she gave each of the dogs a crunchy treat to chew on, they settled into their respective spots on top of her quilt. She draped her robe over a chair, along with her damp slipper socks, and set her glasses aside. Sensing that sleep would remain elusive, either out of fear of the unknown crazy stalking her or curiosity about the US marine who'd made it his mission to make her feel safe tonight, Daisy dropped to her knees and lifted the eyelet dust ruffle to pull her father's old metal tackle box from beneath the bed. She sat on the bed, pulling the quilts over her lap and tucking Muffy against her side before opening the box.

She pushed aside the keepsakes she stored there and pulled out the small stack of letters she'd tied together with a ribbon. Then she propped up the pillows behind her and leaned back to read through Harry's letters again. She held one close to her face to bring the tight, angular handwriting into focus.

Dear Daisy,
Thank you for your letter from 2 May. I hope you are well.

Not that you asked for my opinion, but one of my jobs here is to correct disruptive behaviors. I wouldn't let a man I outranked talk back to me, and you shouldn't let that student talk to you with that kind of language, either. My first instinct would be to shove the ~~jackass~~ young man up against the wall and wash his mouth out with soap. But I suppose your principal and his parents would frown upon that. Are there parents? I had a potty mouth until I got placed with my second set of foster parents. Used to shock ~~the hell out of~~ Hope. (Clearly, I've gotten a little lax. If my pen wasn't about to run out of ink, I'd rewrite this thing so I wasn't swearing in front of you, either.) But if he's not learning it at home, he needs to learn it from you. That student needs to respect your command. Take charge.

I recommend avoiding direct eye contact, not speaking to him unless absolutely necessary, not giving him the attention he's looking for. That works on the dogs I train when we need them to be quiet. I'm not telling you to treat your students like dogs, but I can see that regular, consistent training in expected behaviors would be beneficial to managing a classroom.

We've had a slow week here. It makes me nervous when things get too quiet. Your letter offered a nice reprieve from the tension. Tango appreciated the dog treats, and I enjoyed the cookies. And no, I didn't get the two packages mixed up. (Although Tango did actually have some of both. I think he liked the cookies better.)

Yours truly,
MSgt. H. Lockhart

Daisy was in the middle of her third letter when she drifted off to sleep, surrounded by her dogs and watched over by the mysterious marine who had touched her heart.

Chapter Five

It was a good day to be a teacher. But then, Fridays usually were.

Daisy deposited the holiday-scented hand soap on Mary Gamblin's desk, straightening the gift bag and Secret Santa card before peeking into the hallway to ensure the coast was clear before dashing across to her own classroom to grab her bag and coat. With the gift delivered, her to-do list at school was done. She locked up her room and hurried down to the teachers' lounge. She needed to zip in, grab her mail and get out of here for a couple of hours.

She'd had a busy day, working through lunch with Angelo Logan, dressing up in toga-draped sheets with her sophomore literature class to reenact scenes from *Julius Caesar* and celebrating a stack of vocabulary quizzes that everyone in her composition class had passed. Despite having such a short night's sleep, she'd enjoyed a couple of hours of the deepest slumber she'd had in a long time. When she awakened, she'd rolled over onto a pile of letters strewn around her in the bed and on the floor. Remembering the closeness she'd felt reading Harry's letters, remembering he'd been worried enough about her to keep watch over her house all night, remembering the abundant strength of his arms folding around her, all made her smile. She woke up feeling hopeful, renewed and unafraid to face the day.

With the light of day, Harry's truck was gone. But the feelings remained. While coffee brewed and the dogs ran around the backyard, Daisy had unpacked a few more Christmas decorations and hung them around the house. She wouldn't be putting up a tree until this weekend, but little by little she was getting the rest of the house ready to go for the faculty holiday party. Although she still had no explanation for the snowballs tossed against the side of her house, there had been no more boot prints in her yard beyond Harry's that she needed to worry about, and Daisy was feeling Christmasy again. For a little while last night, she hadn't felt as horribly alone as she usually did in that old house. Harry had offered her enough of a reprieve that she could put her imagination to rest and find her fighting spirit again.

Daisy zipped up her coat and looped her bag over her shoulder, heading down the hallway with a purpose to her step, humming a holiday tune. She was going all out this Christmas, partly because of the party, but mostly because she hated that fear, paranoia and even a little depression were such easy moods to succumb to this time of year. Especially this year, when her mom was celebrating Christmas with her stepfather's family and her creepy Secret

Santa gifts were making December feel like a scary Halloween movie.

She exchanged a wave with her principal, Ryan Hague, as he locked up his office and headed out. He was probably heading home for a quick bite of dinner before coming back to supervise tonight's basketball game with a cross-city rival. Daisy smiled, glad she'd taken the time to hang up the white silk ball decorated with plastic mistletoe in the archway leading into her living room. She wasn't expecting any kissing action herself over the holidays, but Mr. Hague was a newlywed who'd married his second wife over the summer. It would be a fun way to start the Christmas party when he and other staff members arrived with their spouses or dates and she ushered them inside.

The clicking of her boots on the marble floor slowed as she tried to remember the last time she'd been kissed. The memory of Brock's dark head bending toward hers while she pushed his sour breath out of her space gave way to an illusory image of Harry Lockhart's damaged face with all its interesting angles and soulful gray eyes. She didn't suppose he was a mistletoe kind of man, indulging in silly holiday traditions, but that didn't stop her from picturing his mouth sliding over hers and those massive arms gathering her up against his chest again. Daisy's breath caught in her throat and she was suddenly uncomfortably warm inside her coat.

When had her patriotic pen pal become the stuff of her fantasies? She had a feeling she hadn't made a terribly good impression on Harry. He seemed to have a hard time relaxing around her. Although he'd been kind enough to check out her backyard, and set up a guard around her house last night, she didn't have to be psychic to sense the antsy energy coming off him. Without any kind of explanation beyond his obvious injuries or perhaps being an introvert, it was far too easy to suspect that *she* was what made him so uncomfortable.

Other footsteps, heavier and moving faster than her own in the hallway behind her, dragged Daisy out of her thoughts. She peeked over her shoulder and saw Bernie Riley's familiar blue and gold jacket and light brown hair. She nodded a greeting to the tall, lanky man. "Coach."

"Gunderson." He jogged a few steps to catch up and walk beside her. Apparently, he was en route to the teacher's lounge, too. "You coming to the game tonight?"

"I'm working the front gate." Selling tickets, checking passes from the other school's staff. "But I'll try to get into the gym to watch some of it. Are you starting Angelo?"

"That kid's my star point guard. Not as tall as his brother. But faster. Smarter on the court, too."

Speaking of brothers… She knew Bernie was focused on tonight's game, but she had to ask, "Did you get my note about Albert?"

"I did." He stuffed his hands into the pockets of his slacks and chuckled. "So he's your new pet project, huh? Always trying to rescue somebody, aren't you."

Daisy bristled at the condescension hidden behind his teasing tone. "We need to do the best we can for all our students, not just the star athletes."

His long fingers clamped around her upper arm, stopping her. "You're not implying that I only care about the students who play for me, are you?"

She had to tilt her head back, way back, for him to see the glare in her eyes as she tugged her arm from his grip. "We're an academic prep school. We shouldn't have students who are failing English. We're going to lose Albert if we don't do something." She wasn't fond of being grabbed like that, but for a man with Coach Riley's ego, perhaps she'd be smarter to make this request about him. "You know how much Albert loves basketball. He respects you. If you encouraged him to—"

"Did you ever stop to think that maybe *you* were the problem?"

"Me?" Daisy rocked back on her heels, as surprised by the accusation as she'd been to feel his hand on her arm. "What do you mean?"

Bernie shrugged, his gaze checking up and down the hallway before landing on her. "Some of those boys—they're young men, really—aren't comfortable being in your class or working one-on-one with you because, well, they have a crush on you."

"Impossible." How could they? She was more than a decade older than the teenagers. She made them write nearly every day, and most of the novels she taught weren't on any high schooler's must-read list. "Did one of them tell you that? Miss Wadsworth is younger than I am. Prettier, too."

"Yeah, but you're friendlier, funnier. You've got that cool hair vibe going." He flicked at a strand of her hair. "Wasn't this red last year? And you were a blonde when I met you. Like my Stella. The kids like that kind of stuff."

"I have never encouraged any one of them on a personal level. When it comes to teaching I have never been anything but professional with my students." She was appalled to hear that she was any part of the school's gossip mill. "There has never been one complaint filed against me."

Bernie's hands were up in surrender and he was grinning again. "Hey, I'm not accusing you of anything. But when you're a walking hormone, it doesn't take much for a kid to think he's in love with somebody who smiles at him or gives him a good grade. You should hear some of the questions I get in health class."

"About me?"

"About women." He arched his brows in a wry expression. "And sex."

No. *Sex* and Ms. G should not be anywhere together in a sentence where students were concerned.

"You think Albert has a crush on me?" Was that why he'd dropped her class? Or was that the explanation for those sick gifts she'd been receiving? Could the beheaded elf and other disturbing mementos be Albert Logan's idea of expressing his feelings for her? Or expressing his frustration that she didn't return his feelings?

"I don't know. The boys don't usually talk about specifics."

If there were some misplaced emotions going on, she shouldn't try to help Albert personally. But that didn't mean she was giving up on helping the young man succeed. "Encourage him to talk to another teacher, then. You could help him."

Bernie took a step back, shaking his head. "Whoa. I'm not an English teacher."

"Even if he starts turning in his assignments, it'll raise his grades. You can teach him responsibility, can't you?"

Bernie considered her request for a few moments, scratching at the back of his head before replying. "I could use his height back on the team. But I'm so busy this time of year."

Daisy took half a step toward him, encouraged that he would consider her request. "Would you at least promise to talk to him?" When he nodded and turned toward the faculty lounge again, Daisy fell into step beside him. "And if you do find out that he's got the hots for me, will you please remind him that I will never be available to a student in that way. It's not just school policy, it's *my* policy."

Bernie reached over her head to open the door. "I'll sit him down and we'll have a chat."

"Thank you." She had to raise her voice to be heard over the animated conversation inside. Eddie Bosch was regaling a couple of their coworkers with a story while Mary Gamblin ran off copies of work-sheets and Carol Musil sorted through the catalogues in her mailbox. They were laughing at the light-up tie Eddie had gotten from his Secret Santa, and lamenting other unfortunate fashion choices they had made over the years.

So much for making a quick exit. While Bernie joined the conversation, Daisy moved toward the bank of mailboxes, already spying the stack of re-worked papers from a student who'd been serving an in-school suspension. She'd tuck those into her bag and go, knowing she couldn't linger if she wanted enough time to get home to let the dogs out, change into a pair of jeans and get back to school for to-night's game. Dinner would have to be a hot dog from the concession stand.

She was sorting through the papers, making sure they were all there, when Eddie came up beside her. "How did that interview go last night? You got a new tenant?"

Hardly. When the guy had said he'd only move in if she kenneled her dogs or left them outside 24/7, she'd been only too happy to show him the door. "No. But I'm meeting with two more prospects tomorrow."

Bernie pulled down a six-pack of sports drinks with his name and a big bow on it from on top of the mailboxes. "Nice."

Clearly, he was faring better with the gifts he'd been receiving from his Secret Santa. Daisy braced herself and stuck her hand inside her own mailbox, dreading what she might find today. She breathed an audible sigh of relief when she found no surprise packages, which made her feel good enough to elaborate on her answer to Eddie's question. "Mr. Friesen liked everything about the place except for me and my dogs. Didn't think we'd be a good fit."

Eddie laughed. "Probably not. But I think you're on to something, leasing part of that big house. Income property. That's what they call it on TV. I'm thinking about finishing my basement and renting it out. How much are you asking for rent? I'm curious to know if it'd be worth the investment."

But Daisy didn't hear the question. She couldn't hear much of anything over the pulse thundering in her ears. She'd been a fool to think her tormentor would have forgotten her for even one day. There it was, clipped to the bottom of the stack of papers— a plain white envelope with just her name and the usual message, typed onto a Christmas label.

Dear Daisy,
Merry Christmas from your Secret Santa.

"Daisy?"

She ignored both Eddie's prompt and Bernie's effort to join the conversation. "You didn't fill the vacancy at your house? Are you still lookin' for someone to rent that room? I might know a guy. Strictly short term."

She hated that her fingers were shaking as she peeled open the back flap of the envelope. She hated that Eddie, Mary and Carol knew enough about the gifts she'd been receiving that Eddie placed a steadying hand on her shoulder, and the two women stopped their work to watch as she pulled out the enclosed card and opened it.

Suddenly, it hurt to breathe. If she'd been alone, she would have screamed.

The graphic sexual act, although drawn in stick figures, left nothing to the imagination. Neither did the caption beneath the picture. *You and me, bitch. When you least expect it. Merry Christmas to me.*

"You okay?" Eddie asked.

No. She wasn't. But the words wouldn't form.

"Is that from your Secret Santa?" Bernie's height made it far too easy to peer over her shoulder to inspect the defiled holiday card. Daisy crushed it in her fist and stuffed it into the pocket of her coat before he could see the disturbing missive. She didn't need anyone else knowing her fear and shame. "You don't like your gift?"

Daisy tilted her face to Bernie's, thinking for one brief second that his friendly smile was a cruel joke. It took a few seconds longer to realize he hadn't seen the sick drawing and remember that he wasn't one of those close friends who knew about the other gifts.

"What's wrong with it?" Bernie asked. "There's not a gift card in there? Is it empty?"

"I have to get out of here." Daisy shrugged off Eddie's hand and hurried to the door while she wasn't too blind with terror to see it.

Coach Riley cursed behind her. "I need to call my wife. If that bitch is playin' another game—"

"Put a sock in it," Eddie warned before hurrying after her. "Give me ten minutes, Dais. I need to finish entering these grades and then I'll walk you out."

"I don't have ten minutes." She glanced in Eddie's direction without really seeing him. "I need to go home and take care of the dogs before I come back for the game."

"Bernie." Eddie snapped at the tall man and gestured for him to follow her.

Bernie glanced up from the cell phone at his ear. "It's still daylight. But if you want me to walk you out, I guess I can."

"No." Daisy needed to get out to her car so she could scream, and maybe get a hold of her thoughts again. No one had hurt her. This was just about getting under her skin and scaring her. She needed to get away from this place and these people and remember she was strong enough to deal with the fear again. "I'm fine," she lied. "Make your call. I'll see you tonight."

HARRY WAS BEGINNING to wonder if anyone in this neighborhood spent much time looking out their windows and butting into other people's business. Although he knew a lot about staying off the radar when he needed to, he wasn't about to assume that he didn't look like some kind of suspicious figure. He glanced into the rearview mirror to study his reflection. Black cap, scarred face, perpetual scowl? Not suspicious—make that threatening. Unless you got to know him. And maybe even then, that was the impression he made on the civilian world.

But clearly, there was no neighborhood watch on this block because he'd been sitting across from Daisy's house or walking the area for most of the past twenty hours without anyone approaching his truck or calling the police to come check him out. That didn't bode well for anyone else keeping an eye out for the well-being of the purple-tinted hug-meister who lived alone in that big blue house.

He spotted her in his side-view mirror, turning the corner in a mini-SUV. Lime green. Obviously, the woman loved color and couldn't get enough of it in her life. Black and khaki suited him just fine. Maybe that opposing difference in their tastes explained a lot about why he was having such a hard time connecting with her. More than the fact she didn't look like the woman he'd imagined in those letters, her cheerful, touchy-feely, ninety-mile-a-minute personality didn't match the reserved, ladylike angel he'd hoped was going to save him from himself.

But those differences hadn't stopped him from looking out for her. He was certain the shrink he'd talked to earlier this afternoon would say he identified with her isolation. Those early years when it had just been him and Hope in a remote cabin in the Ozarks, when they'd had no idea whether their father was going to come home drunk and angry, or not come home at all, had certainly taught him to be self-sufficient. Had taught him to appreciate the comradeship he'd found in the Corps. But what that little boy wouldn't have given to have a real daddy he could truly depend on, someone who would have looked out for him and Hope. Daisy needed someone reliable in her life. For right now, at least, he was it.

Harry raised his hand to wave as she drove past him. But she didn't see him and he curled his fingers into a fist and drew it back into his lap. Like everyone else in this neighborhood, Daisy was unaware of his presence. She was singing along with the radio or talking to someone on a hands-free phone, as she turned into her driveway and shut down the engine. Why didn't she pull into the garage? Was she waiting for the song or phone call to finish? Was this just a quick stop before she went somewhere else? Should he follow her if she left again? Just how far was he going to take this new let's-spy-on-Daisy hobby of his?

After checking his watch, Harry huddled down inside his coat and waited to get a better idea of her immediate plans before he made that decision.

Maybe this need to keep an eye on her had something to do with the unexpected curiosity that made him want to understand her better. Or maybe his fractured brain needed to resign itself to the differences between imagination and reality so that he could put that ideal Daisy to rest and get on with a new plan for getting himself fit to return to active duty.

Ten minutes later, he sat up straight behind the wheel, wondering how long she was going to sit inside her car.

At fifteen minutes, he got out of his truck and jogged across the street.

Harry walked up her driveway, assuming she'd see him approaching in one of her mirrors. But when he reached the driver's side window, he saw her clutching the steering wheel, resting her head against it. There was no music playing. No phone that he could see. She was unaware of his presence. And he could see her lips moving, muttering something over and over. Was she praying? Angry? Crazy?

Already uneasy with her just sitting in the parked car, Harry rapped his knuckles against the window. "Daisy?"

She screamed in response, sliding toward the center console. Harry stepped back, but pointed to the lock on the door, asking her to open it. He retreated another step into the snow as she shoved the door open and climbed out.

"Damn it, Harry, you need to announce yourself." She slammed the door and swatted his shoulder. Now that she was standing and facing him, he could see she'd been crying. Even her glasses—blue this time, a shade lighter than her eyes—couldn't hide the puffy redness behind the lenses. With a noisy harrumph, she grabbed the front of his coat and pulled him out of the snow bank before venting her emotions with another painless swat. "This is the second time your surprise visits have nearly given me a heart attack. Why don't you call first?"

"I was worried." The suspicion that had brought him out of his truck twisted in his gut at the sight of those crystallized tears drying on her cheeks. "People don't sit in their car for fifteen minutes without going someplace unless something is wrong. Besides, I couldn't call. I don't have your number."

He wasn't going to get it, either. Her little fit of temper vanished with an unladylike curse. "Fifteen minutes? It's been that long?" She opened the door again and reached inside to drag her heavy pink bag over the console. "I have to let the dogs out and then be back at school in an hour. I'd like to eat something and change out of these clothes."

She looped the bag over her shoulder and hiked it onto her hip so she could reach back inside to pull her keys from the ignition. But the bag slipped and the door tried to close, and when she jostled between them a wadded-up card fell out of her pocket and bounced across the concrete to land beside his boot. Harry bent down to pick it up, catching a glimpse of green sparkles in the shape of a Christmas tree and… "What the hell?" He smoothed the wrinkled card stock in his palm, ignoring the pornographic artwork to read the threat typed underneath it. "First you've got some guy peeking in your bedroom window and now this crap? Is it the same guy? Have you gotten other garbage like this from him?"

Dots of pink colored her cheeks and she snatched it away. He'd take that as a yes. She stuffed the card into her pocket and hurried through the back gate.

Harry followed right behind her, demanding answers. "Daisy, where did that come from? Who sent it to you? An angry student?"

"I don't know."

"You don't know who sent you that filth?"

She spun around to face him when she reached the deck. "If I did, don't you think I'd put a stop to it?" She looked down on him from the top step. "What are you doing here, anyway? Don't you have a life?"

He didn't, actually. A wry sigh clouded the air around him. "I'm home on leave for six weeks. I don't have anything to do except hang around Hope's apartment and make her worry. The Corps gives me a job to do every day. Here in Kansas City I'm going nuts. Nothing to do but think and walk and think some more."

"I'm a project for you? A hobby to keep you busy?"

He wondered if that hurtful note of sarcasm in her tone was aimed at him or herself. "You're a friend." The women in those letters was even more important to him. "Something's going on and I can help by keeping an eye on things."

"You've been watching my house all day?"

Except for that hour he'd met with Dr. Polk. "Pretty much. I walked around the neighborhood a little bit. In the daylight, I found where the guy was standing when he used your house for target practice last night." He moved past her up the steps and pointed over to the neighbor's house. "That guy's backyard. I missed the tracks last night because of the shrubs, but once I got over the fence—"

"You trespassed in Mr. Finch's yard?" She joined him at the railing.

Could the threat be that close to home? "You got issues with your neighbor?"

"No. It's just—he's so compulsive about his yard and taking care of things. You didn't knock any leaves off his boxwood bushes, did you? Or dent the top of the fence? Patch dug under the fence last summer, tore up some of the roots—"

"You've got somebody stalking you, Daisy." He pounded his fist against the top of the railing. "I wouldn't worry about the damn shrubbery!"

His outburst shocked her. Hell, he hadn't raised his voice like that for weeks now. Watching her clutch the strap of her bag over her chest and retreat from him, he wished he'd been able to control his frustrated concerns. The dogs were barking inside the mudroom and her back was pressed against the door. Her eyes never left his. "I'm sorry. The last thing I want to do is be the person who scares you." That muscle ticked beneath his eye as he buried the useless rage inside him where it belonged. He put his hands up and stepped back, suspecting where her mind had gone and hating himself for taking her there. "I remember you said your ex was violent. I swear I would never hurt you." He shook his head as he heard the words leave his mouth. "That's probably what your ex said, too."

"Actually…" He held himself still as he waited for her to finish that sentence, praying she didn't believe he was as messed up as the man who'd stabbed her. He prayed even harder that she'd be right. "Brock promised that he *would* hurt me if I left him." She pushed her glasses up at her temple, the action making him think she wanted to make sure she was seeing Harry clearly, evaluating him. "He was too controlling. Obsessive. I had to break it off so I could have a life. Rescue dogs. Stay after school with students. Visit my parents and friends. He was drunk that night he broke into my apartment." She dropped her hand to clutch the strap of her bag again. "He kept his promise."

Harry's hands curled into fists again. With the violence he'd seen, it was far too easy to picture how she'd been hurt. But knowing his response should be his issue, not hers, he blanked the images—both real and imagined—and drew in several breaths of the cold winter air to chill the anger simmering through his veins. "Could he have anything to do with those messages?"

"Brock is in prison."

"You know that for a fact? He doesn't have friends on the outside who might be willing to do some dirty work for him?" Daisy was wilting, like a colorful flower that he'd just sprayed with pesticide. He stuffed his hands into his coat pockets and leaned his hip against the railing, hoping the relaxed posture made him look a little less intimidating, a little more like the friend he meant to be. "Look, I know I'm short on tact and charm, and I've got issues with PTSD that I can't always control. But I protect people for a living. I know how to get a job done. I'm trained to assess the enemy. I know how to scout a perimeter and keep the people I'm guarding safe."

He looked away, needing a break from those searching blue eyes. "Right now, I'm trying to protect you. I'm not bothering anybody by keeping an eye on your place. And clearly, somebody's trying to bother *you*. Let me do this." When she didn't answer, he faced her again. "You said you didn't have anybody."

"You feel you owe me this protection because of those letters?" He wouldn't deny it. But he was here for other reasons, too, ones that were too difficult to put into words right now. "I can't have somebody around me whom I can't trust."

"I'm the man in those letters, Daisy. I promise. You can trust me with your life." Maybe he couldn't promise her anything else, but that much he would guarantee. If she'd let him. "I'm here now. Use me."

She considered his vow for several moments before she nodded. She turned away to unlock the door. "It's been a long day and I'm tired, and I have no time to rest. I'm probably extra sensitive to probing questions and hot tempers." Not to mention receiving that message, which had clearly unnerved her. The dogs darted out, circling around her with wagging tails for a warm greeting. Once they'd been sufficiently petted by their mistress, they trotted over to greet him. Seeing Patch prop his front paws against his thigh and Caliban push his head into Harry's hand while Muffy tried to squeeze between the other two dogs seemed to reassure Daisy more than any words he could utter. "I'd be lying if I said I didn't appreciate you keeping an eye on things. I felt safer last night after you left."

Instincts took over the dogs' need for affection and they trotted down the steps to explore the yard. Harry followed Daisy inside the mudroom and stomped the snow off his boots while she hung her coat and bag on a hook.

But when he pulled off his gloves and watch cap and followed her into the hallway, she stopped him with a hand at the middle of his chest, straightening her arm to keep him from coming any farther into the house. He wasn't used to Daisy needing space. In the twenty-four hours since they'd met face to face, she hadn't once been this eager to put some distance between them. He should relish her backing off from all the touchy-feely stuff that bamboozled him.

But now, it only made him worry. "I thought you were okay with me being here."

She pulled her hand away. "Would you make sure the dogs do their business and get some exercise while I change my clothes?"

Harry hesitated a moment, both in leaving her and in being alone with the dogs. But he'd made a career out of doing what needed to be done. "I can do that."

"Thanks." She reached for his hand and gave it a friendly squeeze. Why hadn't he noticed sooner that she had a beautiful smile?

He reversed the grip to hold on to her when she would have pulled away. "And then you're going to tell me what's going on. I want to know how many other threats you've received and when they started. I need to know your schedule, where you'll be and when, and I need to know if there's anyone you suspect."

Smile killer.

Seemed he had a habit of doing that with this woman.

"Daisy, I…" Another verbal apology didn't seem sufficient. And he couldn't just tell her things would be okay because he knew far too well how *not* okay the world could be. Obeying an impulse that felt as right as it was unexpected, Harry tugged on Daisy's hand, pulling her up against his chest and wrapping his arms around her in one of those hugs she seemed to like so well. He turned his nose against the clinging static of her hair and breathed in that sweet scent that was hers alone.

He patted her back a few times, until he thought he heard a soft giggle. Daisy relaxed against him, slipping her arms beneath his coat and flattening them against his back. She rubbed her palms up and down his spine in strokes that warmed his skin through his sweater and soothed the guilt and concern tensing every muscle. Harry stopped patting and started mimicking the caressing motion up and down her back. He felt pretty lame for not having much experience with comforting embraces, but he felt pretty lucky, too, that Daisy was making the effort to help him improve his skills. And he was a quick study, down to the curve of her hip, up beneath the silken weight of her brown and purple hair.

Idly, Harry wondered how the sensations of curves and gentle heat would change without the ribs of her sweater and wrinkled blouse between his hands and her skin. An interested party stirred behind the zipper of his jeans at the idea of touching Daisy's warm skin. He'd like to kiss her, too, to see if those lips were as soft and luscious as they looked—to find out if they'd respond with the same bold enthusiasm of her hugs or be more like the gentle tutelage of her hands. His whole body thrummed with anticipation as he rubbed his lips against her temple, kissing the earpiece of her glasses before adjusting his aim to press his lips against the warm beat of her pulse there. Daisy's arms tightened around him, aligning her body more perfectly against his. Her breasts pillowed against his chest and the tips beaded into pearls that poked through the layers of clothing separating them, making his palms itch to touch those, too.

"Why do I get the feeling you haven't had much of this kind of contact, Top?" she murmured against his neck. "Which is a shame because you're good at it." She added the undeserved compliment, reminding him that while he'd had sex, he'd never once been in a relationship with a woman. Not long distance and certainly not up close and personal like this.

But this was Daisy, his pen pal angel and long-distance friend, and she was scared. He might even be a big part of what scared her. This wasn't the time to give in to curiosity and crude impulses. Right now, all he needed was for her to be safe.

Reluctantly, he loosened his grip on her, turning his head to kiss the same spot on her hair. But never one to be demure or predictable, Daisy lifted her chin and caught his lips with hers. The kiss was surprising, but not so brief that he didn't have a moment to press his mouth over hers, confirming at least one of his speculations. Her lips were as soft and succulent as he'd imagined. And he wanted to kiss her again.

Daisy dropped back onto her heels and pulled away before he fully acknowledged that impulse. "You gonna be okay?" he asked.

She was smiling again when she nodded, and his chest swelled. Yeah. There was a lot to be said for trading hugs and comfort. He didn't feel quite so guilty about stealing that smile away in the first place.

He tugged his hat back over his short hair and pulled on his gloves. "I'll go take care of the dogs."

Chapter Six

"One hot dog with ketchup and extra relish."

Daisy closed the money box and stamped the hands of the three students who'd paid their fee at her table outside the Central Prep gym, encouraging them to enjoy the games before accepting the dinner Harry offered. "I'm starving. Thank you." She took a big bite, savoring the tangy flavors before nodding toward the bottles of soda in Harry's hands. "You're not hungry?"

"Already finished mine." He set one of the sodas on the table and pulled a paper napkin from the pocket of his jeans. He reached over and wiped a dribble of ketchup and pickle juice from the side of her mouth, showing her the stain on the napkin before she snatched it from his fingers. "Why doesn't it surprise me to discover you have a healthy appetite?"

Daisy turned away, feeling the heat of embarrassment creeping into her cheeks. She wiped her mouth a second time before facing him again. "I haven't eaten since lunch, and that was seven hours ago."

"I'm not criticizing." His bottle hissed as he

twisted the cap and released the carbonation pressure. "Just observing. You don't do anything halfway.
Decorating for Christmas. Hugs. Eating hot dogs."

"Are you sure you're not making fun of me?"
Daisy took a daintier bite this time.

"No, ma'am."

She arched an eyebrow. "We talked about that,
Master Sergeant."

"Ouch." For a split second, his stiff mouth crooked
into a smile. But then there was a big roar from the
crowd in the gym as someone on the junior varsity
team made an exciting play. Harry's alert gaze darted
through the doorway toward the bleachers. A muscle tightened across his angular cheekbone before
he swallowed a drink of soda and brought his gaze
back to hers. "No more fancy titles for you and me.
In my defense, though, we are back at school. Tech-
nically, you're on duty."

Daisy wadded up her napkin and tossed it at him.
He deftly caught it and tossed it into the trash can
beside the table. Although this familiar camaraderie
had settled between them, not unlike the conversation they'd shared in their long-distance letters, Daisy
felt raw inside. Harry had insisted he drive her to
school, and for a man so averse to long conversations, he'd had plenty of questions to ask about her
Secret Santa. At his insistence, she'd unlocked her
classroom to show him the gifts hidden inside her
desk, as well as her mailbox in the teachers' lounge
where most of the messages and gifts had been delivered. Seemingly immune to the curious stares at

his scarred face, he'd asked her to introduce him to several coworkers, glossing over thank-yous for his service to the country and turning the conversations around to learn a little more about Principal Hague, Eddie Bosch and Mary Gamblin.

Despite security protocols that were in place to protect the school from outside threats, access to her inside the school was too easy, he'd complained. And she was too isolated at home for him to deem either place safe. Although she'd teased him about his natural talent for bringing down the mood of a room, the underlying truth to his words had left her feeling unsettled. His advice that she be hypervigilant to her surroundings, avoid being alone or even one-on-one with any of the male students or faculty in the building, and report anyone lurking near her classroom or faculty workroom to the principal made her that much more edgy and distrustful of the people she interacted with nearly every day of her life.

Two weeks ago, before the first message had been delivered, she'd been content to surround herself with students and work. She was a social creature by nature. She was proud of her school, liked her students and coworkers, reveled in the holiday season, loved being busy and doing for others.

But tonight, despite her spirited blue and gold facade, all she wanted was to go home to her dogs and lock her doors. She couldn't say whether it was Harry's reserved, imposing presence, casting suspicion in a wide net around her, or the fact this damaged yet fit, virile man was enduring his aversion to the crowd to not only protect her, but to also be kind to her, that left her feeling so off-kilter this evening.

"Daisy."

She hadn't realized how far into her troubling thoughts she'd sunk until Harry spoke her name and nodded toward the group jostling for position on the opposite side of the table.

Complete with two sets of grandparents, two elementary-aged children and a curly-haired toddler who was fussing to climb down from her mother's arms and explore, the family's arrival required Daisy to focus on her job. After calculating the discounts, she gave them the price for their tickets, even splitting the cost in half for them when both grandfathers insisted on paying.

By the time she finished counting back their change and stamping hands, Daisy realized the little girl had stopped squirming and was staring at Harry. Harry was staring right back. In that grim, clenched-jaw look that made the muscle beneath his right eye spasm. The little girl smiled and pointed at Harry. "Bomba No-man."

"Abominable Snowman?" The mother saw where her daughter was pointing, and pulled her hand away. "I'm sorry. You must remind her of a character in one of those animated Christmas shows she watches."

"Not a problem, ma'am," Harry reassured her. "I've been called worse."

But it *was* a problem. Even as the family moved into the gym to find seats on the bleachers, Harry was retreating against the cinder block wall behind him. She heard the plastic of his soda bottle cracking as he squeezed it in his hand.

However, pointing out the disfiguring scars didn't seem to bother him as much as the noise. The referees blew their whistles and the timeout buzzer sounded. The pep band struck up an enthusiastic rendition of the school fight song. That muscle ticked across Harry's cheek and he turned his head as if the cacophony hurt his ears.

"Are you okay?" She took a drink, trying to hide how much his charged, yet overtly still, posture worried her. She gestured to the metal chair beside hers. "You can sit if you want."

"I'm better standing." So he could make a quicker getaway if he had to, no doubt.

With no one waiting in line for tickets, Daisy sat on the edge of the table, facing him. "You said you suffer from PTSD. Do the loud noises bother you?

Harry's dark gray eyes scanned the lobby, from the glimpse inside the gym to the line waiting at the concession stand. "A basketball game is not going to make me freak out."

"But other things will?"

His gaze landed on her. He hesitated a moment before dropping his volume and answering. "Sometimes a loud bang will trigger memories. Your dogs charging at me last night kind of…" He twirled his fingers beside his head, indicating some kind of flashback, she supposed. "Usually it's the smells that are the worst."

"Like what?" More than once, she'd caught him

sniffing her hair. And she'd already memorized his unique scent, undoctored by any aftershave or cologne. He must be particularly sensitive to certain odors. "Do you smell anything here?"

He rolled his shoulders as if his sweater was suddenly uncomfortably tight. "This isn't the place for that kind of conversation."

"Maybe when we get home. You could stay for a while." Daisy pushed to her feet, needing to touch him to comfort him somehow. She reached for his free hand and squeezed his fingers. "Do you need to talk about it? I could make us some hot chocolate and stay up as late as you need to. You mentioned things in your letters—like you needed to get them off your chest. I don't claim to understand everything you've been through, but I do know a little about how horrible the world can be."

He stared at her hard for a moment, muttering something about an angel that she couldn't quite make out over the squeaks of rubber-soled shoes on the polished gymnasium floor.

"I've got a therapist for those kinds of talks." Harry's grip pulsed around her hand. "I'm not interested in making you cry anymore."

Daisy leaned in, matching his hushed tone. "Even if I did, it would be all right. If I can help… I want to."

"Are you asking this guy for a favor, too?"

Recognizing the smug woman's voice behind her, Daisy plopped her forehead against Harry's chest for a moment and audibly groaned. Then she released his hand and turned to the statuesque blonde in a coat most likely from a pricey boutique. "Excuse me?"

Stella Riley, resident trophy wife and all-around ego buster as far as Daisy was concerned. Stella grinned, waving off what had sounded like an accusation. "I'm just teasing. Bernie said you'd asked for his help."

"With a student."

"Is this your new gentleman friend? Bernie thought you might have met someone, but that you were keeping him a secret." The woman extended her hand across the table. "Hi. I'm Stella, Coach Riley's wife."

"Basketball coach," Daisy whispered, explaining the pronouncement. While part of her wanted to correct the assumption that Harry was her boyfriend, she also knew this conversation would end sooner if she just let Stella say what she wanted to and move on.

Daisy startled at the brush of Harry's fingers against the small of her back. Was he reassuring her? Or grounding himself? He tossed his empty bottle into the trash before shaking Stella's hand. "Harry Lockhart."

"Military, right?"

"Yes, ma'am. Marine Corps."

"I could tell by the haircut." She winked before releasing him. "It suits you. We're proud of you boys. And we're all glad that Daisy has found someone again." Stella pulled her ID card out of her wallet and flashed it at Daisy. "Not that you need this to know who I am. But I want to follow the rules."

"You're good to go, Stella." Daisy had a hard time zeroing in on Stella's name on the list of faculty and spouses who got in free because Harry's palm had slipped beneath the hem of her gold cardigan and flattened against her back. Daisy felt the brand of his touch through her blouse as surely as the stamp she inked onto Stella's hand.

Stella tipped her blond curls toward the gym. "How's it going?"

"I haven't been able to check the score yet, but there's lots of cheering, so I'm guessing pretty well."

"Great. Bernie will be in a good mood, then." Stella's wave included both Harry and Daisy. "Nice to meet you, soldier boy. Don't be a stranger. I'll see you next week, Daisy. If you need any help with the party, let me know."

"That was like a tornado blowing through," Harry muttered, absentmindedly rubbing his hand in small circles against her spine. "Is she a friend of yours?"

Whether soothing her taut nerves or assuaging his own, Daisy had to step away from his distracting touch so she could think of words to speak. "She *is* first lady of the basketball court. When the team has a winning season, I guess she deserves some of the credit, too."

"You didn't answer my question."

"I work with her husband."

"Still not an answer." Daisy busied herself straightening the items on the table. "You know, other people say bad things about people. You're too big-hearted to do that, aren't you? The fact that you won't makes me think there's some friction between you and the first lady."

Daisy stopped her busy work. "I never have understood people who think they're all that. It feels like I'm back in high school whenever I'm around her. Of course, maybe if I'd been one of the popular kids back then instead of an artsy geek, I might feel differently."

"Still avoiding the question, Ms. Geek."

"I liked you better when you wouldn't talk to me."

Harry laughed. Although far too brief, his laugh was a rich, chest-deep sound that made her smile. She adjusted her glasses to see the pliant side of his mouth smiling, too.

A hundred little wishes locked up inside her heart unfurled at the knowledge she'd put that smile there. "Maybe her snootiness stems from insecurity. I imagine she's alone a lot during basketball season with all the games and practices. Sometimes, I think she's jealous that other people get to spend more time with her husband than she does."

Harry's smile vanished as quickly as it had appeared. "How jealous?"

"Jealous enough to send me those threats?" Daisy shook her head. While she'd never felt especially comfortable around Stella Riley, she couldn't see any reason for the woman to have a personal grudge against her. "Those have to be from a guy. Right?"

Harry wasn't probing for answers anymore. He

was moving to intercept the tall young black man who circled around the table.

"Now you got Coach Riley callin' my granny on me?" Albert Logan's Central Prep ball cap was cocked off to the side, giving him a deceptively juvenile look. But there was nothing childlike about the anger in his expression. "Ain't 'Lo man enough for you? You want to give me some private tutoring, too? Let's do it, Ms. G."

Daisy planted her feet, cringing at his grammar and hating the innuendo in his tone. "Not if you're going to talk to me like that. I'll report you to Mr. Hague. This isn't a punishment. We're concerned about you, Albert."

"You stay out of my business, or I'm gonna get all up in yours."

The moment Albert's pointing finger got too close, Harry palmed the teenager's shoulder and pushed him away, sliding between her and Albert.

Albert knocked the restraining hand away. "Get your hands off me, old man."

Harry squared off against the bigger, younger man. Although she couldn't see Harry's face, she could read every wary line of tension in his muscular stance. There were rules against touching students. Harry wasn't staff, but this standoff could escalate in a heartbeat if he thought he had to protect her.

"It's okay, Harry." She closed her hand over his rock-hard bicep, knowing she had to reach him with words and touch because there'd be no way she could physically restrain him. She splayed her other hand against his back, remembering how distracting his touch had been to her just a few minutes earlier. "This is Albert Logan, a former student of mine." With Harry's hands fisting at his sides, she appealed to Albert, as well. "Master Sergeant Lockhart is my pen pal from last year's writing project. He's home on leave."

"Take a step back," Harry warned. His muscles vibrated with tension beneath her fingers.

"Albert, please. I don't want to call the principal."

Albert glanced back and forth between the two of them, considering how a confrontation with Harry would play out, then wisely decided to retreat a step. Curiosity replaced the wounded pride and anger that had puffed up his posture, reminding Daisy that in many ways, these nearly grown students were still just big kids. Albert rubbed his knuckles across his cheek. "Dude, did that happen to you over there?"

The poised wariness didn't waver. "Yes."

"Was it a car bomb?"

"Albert…"

Picking up on subtle clues had never been Albert's strong suit. "You know Corporal Benny Garcia?" he asked. "That's the guy I wrote to. When I still had Ms. G for class. He drove one of those armored cars."

"I knew Garcia." *Knew?* Harry's shoulders lifted with a deep breath. "He drove an LAV—Light Armored Vehicle."

Compassion squeezed Daisy's heart. Was Albert hearing any of those past-tense references? She curled her fingers into the back of Harry's sweater, wishing they were in a less public place so she could wind her arms around his waist.

"Yeah. He used a bunch of initials I didn't understand. But it was cool when he talked about the motor and stuff." Albert's dark gaze suddenly shifted to her. "Angelo know you got a boyfriend, Ms. G?"

Why was everyone assuming that she and Harry were an item? Then she saw the way she had latched on to Harry, and the way he'd blocked her into a corner between the table and wall, defending her. Was there some unacknowledged longing she was projecting out into the universe that everyone but her could see?

"Who is Angelo?"

Albert dragged his focus back to Harry. "'Lo's my brother. He's playing tonight. He and Ms. G... He..." He glanced to her, looking for what? He knew exactly what kind of relationship she had with his brother. Was he hinting at something else? "Uh..."

"I'm helping Angelo with his scholarship applications. He's one of my best students. I think Albert could be, too."

Apparently satisfied with Albert's family history, Harry gave a curt nod and switched topics. "Where I come from, a man doesn't wear his cover inside. His hat," he explained, when Albert frowned. "And he speaks to a woman with respect. I suggest you do the same."

Albert shrugged. "Okay."

"Okay, what?"

"Okay, sir?"

Harry eyed the sideways hat until Albert pulled it off and stuffed the brim in the back pocket of his jeans. "Now we understand each other."

Instead of acting chastised, Albert grinned. "Benny said you were a tough son-of-a..." He glanced at Daisy, watched Harry's stance change, and thought better of finishing that phrase. "Benny respects you, sir."

"It was mutual."

Albert looked at Daisy and shrugged. "Sorry, Ms. G. Granny said I had to check in with you Monday before I go to work. Just don't call her no more."

"Anymore," Daisy automatically corrected.

"Yeah. She's scarier than both of you put together." The whole confrontation forgotten, Albert whistled to a couple of friends and joined them in line at the concession stand.

Harry dropped his gaze where her hand still clung to his arm. "Afraid I was going to take him out?"

She released her grip. "Were you?"

"I know I'm not surrounded by insurgents." His breathing seemed a little labored, though, when he faced her. "But you don't let them get close like that unless you know them. I didn't know that kid. The way he was coming at you..."

She wanted to ask about Corporal Garcia, find out if he'd lost his friend in an enemy attack. She desperately wanted to wind her arms around him and hold on until that tightly leashed tension quaking through his body eased.

But the buzzer sounded, marking the end of

the first basketball game. Fans cheered. The band played again, loud even to her own ears. A swarm of students and families spilled through the archway, flooding the lobby between the JV and varsity games. Harry muttered the very curse he'd kept Albert from saying and grabbed his coat from beneath the table.

"Are you okay?" Daisy moved to keep his face in sight, worried he was having some kind of meltdown. "This is too much for you, isn't it."

"I need some fresh air." He was struggling. His eyes were clear, but they locked on to hers while he zipped up, as if focusing on her, and not the people gathering in the space around them, centered him. Fine. She'd be still and let him focus. "I better call Hope and let her know where I am. She worries more than she needs to, and that's not good for the baby. Besides, I'd like to familiarize myself with the layout of the school grounds. I want to know every way somebody could get in or out."

Daisy understood his sister's need to worry. She sensed it was taking every bit of strength he had not to explode. "Will you be coming back?"

"I'm your ride home, aren't I? I just need to move. I'll probably run a couple laps around the building."

"Through the snow?"

"I like the cold." His fingers were unsteady when he threaded them into the hair at her temple and smoothed the waves down behind her ear. He cupped the side of her neck and jaw, and the trembling stilled. Daisy turned into his touch. With his heat warming her skin, her concerns ebbed to a less frantic pitch, and she hoped he was taking at least the same from her. "When you're ready to leave, go to the front door. I'll watch for you. You don't step foot outside until I'm here to walk you out, okay?"

"Okay."

His fingertips tightened against her skin. "I mean it, Dais."

She smiled. "Okay, *sir.*"

His eyes widened for a split second at her sass. And then he was leaning in, kissing her. The press of his lips was firm, their movement stilted, but urgent enough to demand her response. The tip of his tongue moistened the point of contact between them with a raspy caress, but retreated before she could catch it. Harry's kiss was not quite chaste and over far too quick. Slightly breathless, she was still clinging to his bottom lip when he pulled away. His eyes had darkened like charcoal, and she wondered which of them was swaying on their feet.

Without a word, Harry released his grip and turned away. He darted through the crowd and disappeared out the double front doors into the night.

PDA might be frowned upon on school property, but Daisy wasn't complaining. The warmth of that surprising kiss stayed with her the rest of the evening. And though she kept one eye on the door, even when she stood in the archway to watch the last few minutes of the second game, Harry never came back. She hoped he'd snuck in to get some hot coffee instead of waiting for her out in the cold for an hour.

But she was half afraid that the run-in with Albert, the noise and energy of the crowd, or even the kiss itself had frightened him off.

She had no doubts that he was still out there, waiting to drive her home, making sure she was safe. But she was sad for him that it was so hard to relax and enjoy himself for very long. And she was antsy to get back to him to see if they could recreate a little of that one-on-one magic where they joked with each other, and touched and cared and kissed.

That was why Daisy had the money counted down and locked up inside the office before the final buzzer sounded. While the building cleared, she did a quick walk-through of the gymnasium bleachers with Eddie and Mary, picking up trash while the custodian swept the floor. She kept her distance from the heated conversation between Bernie and Stella Riley outside the boys' locker room, quickly diverting her attention when both their gazes landed on her. "What did I do?" she whispered to Eddie before dumping the stack of paper cups she'd collected into the trash bag he carried.

"Who knows?" Eddie shrugged. "Sometimes I think that woman's even jealous of me. And Bernie's certainly not *my* type."

Daisy wanted to laugh, but couldn't. "That's sad that she's so insecure. I know Bernie's got an ego the size of Arrowhead Stadium, but has he ever really cheated on her?"

Mary climbed down the bleachers to add her trash

to the bag. "I heard that she's the one who cheated on him, in college, before they got married."

Daisy tuned out the bickering couple and headed toward the lobby. "Whatever their issues are, I wish they'd leave me out of it."

The band parents who'd been working the concession stand for their booster club fundraiser had cleaned up their area and locked the serving window partition by the time she said goodbye to Eddie and Mary. Eddie made sure Harry was still there to drive her home before escorting Mary out to her car. Mr. Hague was doing a walk-around to make sure all the doors were locked. The players and the opposing team members would leave by the locker room entrance. Daisy was alone in the lobby when she realized the chairs and table from gate duty had been left out.

It wouldn't take her five minutes to fold up the chairs and take them down to the basement storage room. The table would be a two-person project to carry down the steps, but by the time she put away the folding chairs, either the custodian would be finished or Mr. Hague would be back, and they could help. Then she'd be done with her assignment and she could get to Harry and that private conversation and maybe even another kiss.

She stuck her keys into the pocket of her jeans, then pulled out her phone. She had a split-second idea to call Harry in to have him help her, but just as quickly she realized she didn't have his number. Was it too late to call Hope and ask for it? That seemed silly when it'd be quicker to run outside and ask Harry herself. But he'd insisted that she not leave the building without him. He said he'd be watching the front doors. She could step outside and wave...

"Stop overthinking this, Daisy Lou." She stuffed her phone into another pocket. "Just finish up and go."

Tossing her coat over her bag, she picked up the chairs. Using one of her school keys, she unlocked the metal gate blocking off the stairs from the public and pushed it open. She carried the folding chairs down the concrete steps and descended half a century into the past. The long gray hallway was broken up by four heavy steel doors. Hung on runners like an old barn door, these doors simply unlatched and slid open. After the boiler room, the rest of the doors led to old classrooms from the original building before state regulations and a school improvement bond had required a new facility be built around the old one. With the original windows enclosed by new construction, the storage rooms doubled as tornado shelters now.

She pulled on the latch of the second metal door and shoved it off to the right, cringing at the grinding whine of metal on metal. The keyless latches were a throwback to the original building, too, before terrorists and school shootings made it vital that every school could be locked down to keep intruders out. After flipping on the light switch, she carried the chairs over to the closest of several racks lined up against the far wall. After setting the chairs into place, Daisy glanced around her. Metal racks with metal chairs. Gray concrete walls. In a basement. With no windows.

She shivered. This level was uninviting enough in the daytime. No natural light. No color. No warmth. At night, it felt even colder, despite the boiler room cranking out heat next door. If she ever had to teach a full day down here in this tomb, the powers that be would be carrying her out in a straitjacket. She was more than happy to pay a few extra cents on her taxes to have two whole floors of bright, well-lit rooms above her.

Metal grated against metal behind her. Daisy turned to see the last few inches of hallway disappear as the door slammed with an ominous clank. "Hey! I'm in here."

She heard a second clank as she dashed across the room.

What was going on? Daisy pushed on the latch and stumbled into the door when nothing happened. "No," she whispered, pumping the latch a half dozen times with the same result. Nothing was catching inside the locking mechanism to release the door. She pulled on the latch even though the metal clearly said *Push*. She tried sliding the door along its runner, in case the latch was the only problem. But the heavy steel wasn't budging. "This isn't funny," she yelled, slapping the flat of her hand against the door.

She was locked in.

Had the custodian or Mr. Hague not seen the light and carelessly closed the door? Was this a practical joke? Not funny. She pounded on the door, pushed the broken latch. "Let me out of here!"

Daisy drifted back a step, feeling suddenly light-headed. Could someone have locked her in on purpose?

Then she heard noises that locked her breath up in her chest and turned her blood to ice.

Scratching against the metal. Something heavy being dragged across the floor. Someone breathing harder with the exertion. Whoever had locked her in was still there.

Her Secret Santa.

"Who are you?" she demanded. A pungent odor stung her nose. "Why are you doing this to me?"

She backed away even farther when the person on the other side refused to respond. Tamping down the fear that scattered her thoughts, she remembered her cell and pulled it from her pocket. "I'm calling the police," she warned.

As soon as the screen lit up, she said a prayer of thanks for good cell service and punched in 9-1-1.

Everything went quiet on the other side of the door as the call connected. "That's right. *You* be afraid this time."

But her bravado was short-lived.

The silent person on the other side nudged a familiar piece of cardstock beneath the door at her feet. White, with a sparkly green Christmas tree, and three words staring up at her.

Ho. Ho. Ho.

The 9-1-1 dispatcher answered the call, but Daisy couldn't speak.

The sick torment of another message wasn't the only thing coming from beneath the door.

Daisy blinked away the tears burning her eyes.

Smoke.

Chapter Seven

Harry rubbed his gloved hands together, keeping them warm as the visiting team's bus left the parking lot. He was more of a football guy than a basketball fan, but he knew enough about high-school sports to know the players and their coaches were generally the last people to leave the building. He bounced on the balls of his feet as two more cars followed the bus onto the main road. That left just his truck, a van and two other vehicles in the nearly empty parking lot.

"Come on, Daisy."

The images of how some sicko wanted to hurt her made his skin crawl. The bad joke gifts, graphic pictures and Peeping Tom all said coward to him. Daisy's stalker wasn't brave enough to confront her face-to-face. But he sure seemed to be getting off on scaring her, on watching her from afar and savoring how his psychological terror campaign controlled her life. He didn't understand enough about profiling to know whether her stalker had some skewed idea of love for her, or if this obsession was some kind of punishment.

But a coward like that could become unpredictable in a heartbeat if he thought his control over her was slipping—just like Daisy's ex. She'd been brutally honest in one of her letters about the night her ex had come after her with a knife. She'd wanted Harry to know that she could deal with the things he'd shared with her, that she was a survivor and that she was stronger for it. But a woman like Daisy, with such zest for people and life, should never be punished or controlled like that. Acid churned in the pit of his stomach at the thought of someone hurting her like that again.

He'd never thought he'd be stepping up for guard duty for a chatty, compassionate free spirit. For months now, he'd focused solely on fixing himself— and that project wasn't complete yet. Did he really think he had what it took to keep Daisy safe?

Like right now, Harry had a bad feeling about the number of vehicles left in the parking lot.

But then he was the one whose head wasn't on straight. He had a bad feeling about almost everything these days, seeing an enemy where there was none. He knew the van belonged to the custodian on duty tonight because the guy had come out for a cigarette during the second game. The well-appointed Cadillac must belong to the principal. Harry had seen him at more than one door, locking up. The other car could be abandoned for all he knew. It had a yellow sticker on the windshield, so it belonged to someone who worked at or went to the school.

He stopped at the front of his truck again. Although he couldn't see any movement through the bank of glass doors at the front of the building, the lights were still on inside the lobby and gymnasium, so chances were that Daisy was just fine.

He probably shouldn't have left her alone for this long. But the crowd and cheers and drums had been too much for him. That kid, Albert, had been ticked off with Daisy. Wounded pride over some school problem. Harry's instinct was to intervene—to keep the danger at bay before he had to become a part of it. But then Albert had mentioned Benny Garcia, and that had taken him right back to the middle of that last firefight, and he knew he was losing it.

Lt. Col. Biro was right. He wasn't much use to anybody in this condition. A wounded warrior. Damaged goods. He had a Purple Heart and a Silver Star, but he couldn't handle teenage smart-assery and a noisy basketball game.

If he was at Hope's apartment with his duffel bag, he'd be pulling out one of Daisy's letters right about now. He'd read her words and feel her caring. He'd cool his jets and come back to the normal land of the living. At least, as normal as he could get.

This time, instead of reading the words and letting his angel lift him out of his mental hellhole, Harry's thoughts drifted back to myopic blue eyes and a beautiful smile. The real Daisy Gunderson was a far cry from the woman he'd imagined. But different meant just that—not any better or worse. And *different* hadn't stopped him when the noise and the stress had gotten to be too much, and he'd anchored his senses on her luscious, irresistible mouth. He'd kissed her. Not a peck on the lips like the thank-you she'd given him at her house that afternoon. A real kiss. He hadn't been sure he could still kiss a woman. But the need had been too powerful to resist.

He hoped his damaged nerves and scar tissue hadn't completely grossed her out because Daisy had been wonderful. He'd felt her mouth soften under his. He'd tasted her. He'd felt her response through every surviving nerve ending and deeper inside in places that had nothing to do with nerves.

Selfishly saving himself by coming to Kansas City and meeting her in person had become doing a favor for a friend. And now looking out for Daisy was becoming something…selfish again. So much for putting his ideal Ms. G. up on a pedestal. For a few blissful seconds, he'd forgotten everything except his desire to kiss that beautiful mouth.

A smoother operator in a less public place would have deepened that kiss. A man who was a little less *abominable* and little more sure this unplanned attraction he felt was mutual would have pulled Daisy into his arms and pushed her up against that wall to feel every inch of those curves and grasping hands while he plundered her heavenly soft mouth. Those unexpectedly heated thoughts about all the ways he wanted to kiss Daisy had required a third hike through the snow to ease the ill-timed fantasies about the earthy, purple-haired temptress and the embarrassing hard-on they'd aroused.

He hadn't felt like that much of a man in months.

He hadn't felt that kind of normal. He hadn't felt such a deep connection to another human being since opening that first letter overseas all those months ago.

And already he felt like that connection was fading.

"Come to the damn door, woman." The wintry night air was moving past being a healing remedy and was becoming a nose-numbing reminder that he'd been out here far too long without having any contact with her.

Harry pulled out his phone to call her and swore. He'd known Daisy for almost a year and a half and had been with her most of the past twenty-four hours—and he'd never once remembered to get her phone number. Not very slick. Or practical.

He was scrolling through information on his phone, looking for the Central Prep Academy number when he heard the first siren in the distance.

If an empty parking lot had given him a bad feeling, the sinuous noise of two more sirens cutting through the crisp night air was telling him to trust that feeling. "Daisy?"

A shrill, uninterrupted ringing from a much closer source jerked him around. Fire alarm. "Daisy!"

He needed her with him. Now.

Harry pulled a crowbar from the toolbox behind the seat of his truck. He ran to the front doors, tried two of them, but they were both locked. He didn't bother with the third or fourth door. He jammed the crowbar between the door and frame and forced it open. He'd probably just triggered another alarm in the office or at a nearby police station. But he knew he could use the backup the moment the door swung open and he dashed through the vestibule. A thin, gray haze hung in the air, stinging his sinuses with the distinctive smell of smoke. The memory of an explosion went off inside his head, but he clenched his jaw, forbidding the nightmare to seize hold of his thoughts. No Tango. No bomb. He was home in Kansas City. The damn school was on fire and Daisy was in it.

Harry surveyed the lobby and saw no one, just a folded-up table with Daisy's pink purse hidden behind it. He found the custodian inside the gym on his cell phone, talking to a dispatcher. Harry waved him toward the front doors, ordering him to report that there were at least two other people inside the building.

Then he followed the hazy wisps of toxic fumes to the top of a stairwell where a darker cloud of smoke was gathering beneath his feet. He inspected the open padlock and gate, heard the distinctive whoosh and pops of live flames. The smoke swirled around his ankles as he went partway down the steps. "Daisy? Daisy Gunderson, are you down here?"

His answer was a couple of loud bangs, a muffled curse and then a croaky, "Harry? I'm trapped. There's smoke. I called 9-1-1. I pulled the fire alarm in here."

Smart woman. Harry took the stairs two at a time, running straight at the sound of her voice. "I heard the sirens. The fire department is on its way." The smoke was denser down here, the breathable air more pungent. There was nothing accidental about this blaze. The fire itself was a small pyre in the middle of the hallway, piled with rags, a bag of trash and what looked like a woman's coat, all shriveling into ash and goo as they burned and melted. The concrete and metal down here would be hard to burn, but he smelled enough acetone, probably varnish or paint solvent, to make his eyes water. He shoved open the first door and discovered the boiler room. "Daisy?"

He heard her coughing again and kept moving. Metal banged against metal. "In here."

The next door. Right beside the blaze. With more accelerant splashed on the door itself so that rivulets of fire ran down the heavy steel.

"Hang on, honey, I'm coming." Harry edged around the puddle of flames dripping on the floor to get his hand on the door, but he quickly snatched it away. Even through the leather and lining of his glove, the rising temperature scorched him. "Don't touch the door," he warned. "It's hot."

"That's why I've been hitting it with this metal chair." Her brave voice stuttered with another fit of coughing. "I can't get it open."

He couldn't, either, unless he could put out some of those flames and get closer. He swung his gaze around. Through the chimeras of heat rising toward the ceiling, Harry caught a glimpse of a ghostly figure climbing the stairs at the far end of the long corridor. Was that a trick of the smoke? A flashback to

tracking insurgents in that village outside Fallujah?
The instinct to give chase to the potential enemy
tensed through every muscle. "Hey!" he shouted.
"Stop!"

"What is it?" Daisy gasped.

The apparition was gone. The reality was here.
"Nothing. Never mind."

"He's jammed the door or broken the lock." Daisy's coughing reminded Harry that his priority was
to keep her safe. That meant finding a way to get
her out of there.

He spotted the fire extinguisher cabinet anchored
to the wall. On the other side of the fire. "Are you
hurt?" Harry asked, using the crowbar to shove the
center point of that fire, a heavy bucket that was
melting with the heat, off to one side. The bucket
tipped, and more flames shot out across the floor.
But in that split second the fire was moving away
from him and the door, Harry darted past.

"I burned my hand on the door, but it's not serious. It's getting harder to breathe."

He couldn't breathe. The old memories snuck
around his defenses, blending with reality. *Tango
had hit on something. He knew that dog's reactions
the way he knew his own thoughts. Harry raised his
fist, warning his patrol to stop their advance.* "What
is it, boy? Show me." *He heard the thwap of the bullet and watched Tango fall.* "Tango!" *Harry's world
exploded around him. IED. The dog had known. He
ran toward the heat. He couldn't leave his partner
behind.* "Top, you got to leave him! We have to re-

treat!" He jerked his arm away and raised his rifle, charging toward his downed partner when the second blast hit.

"Harry?" It was a woman's voice calling his name. Daisy's voice. "Harry, are you still there?"

Do this, Marine!

Harry swore, forcing himself into the present. He ducked his head and swung the crowbar, shattering the glass in front of the fire extinguisher.

"I'm here, honey." Harry pulled the pin and fired a stream of foam into the flames, dousing a path before aiming the extinguisher at the door itself. "I'm going to get you out."

The sting of the burning chemical was in his eyes now. The toxic air tickled his throat and filtered into his lungs. The heat from the flames themselves had puckered every pore in his skin, making him feel like his boots and clothes were melting. The foam trickled down the door, taking the flames with it. Every new inch revealed burnt streaks and blistered paint and a single word etched into the metal itself. *Mine.*

A rage as hot as the fire itself seared through Harry's brain. How could one person be so sick in the head that he would want to hurt a woman with a heart as big as Daisy's? He turned down the smoke-filled hallway. He should have run down that SOB. He didn't need to be armed to take a man down. He could have put a stop to this insane terror campaign once and for all.

"Harry, please." She was coughing again.

Stay focused on the mission, Top. Harry tossed

the extinguisher aside and picked up the crowbar. "Stand back. When I open this, it may suction the flames into the room."

"I'm ready."

The latch was busted, useless. This was going to take brute force. Finally. Something he could manage without thinking twice. Harry wedged the crowbar between the door and wall and pushed against it, then pulled back, roaring with the strain through his arms and shoulders before the warping metal finally gave way. Once he'd moved the door a couple of inches, he dropped the crowbar and muscled the hanging door across its track. He was coughing now, too. "Daisy?"

"Harry!" She launched herself against his chest, heedless of the flames licking into the room she'd just vacated. He cinched an arm around her waist and turned her away from the conflagration, carrying her several feet beyond the worst of the fire. He felt her lips press against his damaged cheek and jaw again and again. "Thank you. Thank… Oh, my God."

Harry turned her away from the hateful epithet and tried to keep moving. But she squiggled in his grasp, wanting to see. "Did you see him? Was that who you were yelling at? Who was it? Is that my coat? Why would he—?"

"I didn't get a good look." Her body shook with another fit of coughing and he tried to pick her up. "Keep your head down. The smoke is getting thick."

"He slipped a card under the door. We need it for evidence."

She batted his hands away, turning sideways against him, although he wasn't letting her get any closer to the blaze. "No you don't. The cops will know this was intentional."

"There may be fingerprints."

"No."

"I heard the scratching. He was carving…" Her toes touched the floor, tangling with his feet. He lost his grip as they stumbled into the wall. She fought with him, struggling to get a better view of the destruction. "…that. *Mine?* I belong to him? He owns something I need to stay away from?"

He grasped her shoulders. "We have to move."

"He must have been watching, waiting until I was—"

"Stop talking and get your butt moving!" Daisy flinched away from him, her red-rimmed eyes wide behind her glasses as she clutched at the wall instead of him. Harry heard his voice echoing through the hallway and truly understood why Lt. Col. Biro had been so worried about his ability to serve. "I'm sorry." He backed away to the opposite wall, his hands raised in apology. He'd just yelled in her face as if she was a raw recruit. As if he wasn't any better than that bastard who'd hurt her. The fumes rubbed like grit in his eyes. "My head's not right. I didn't mean that. Don't… Don't ever stop talking to me. Please."

And then that woman did the most remarkable thing. She pushed away from the wall, grabbed the front of his coat and dragged him toward the stairs.

"Get me out of here, Top," she ordered. "We both need fresh air."

When she doubled over in another coughing jag, Harry's training took over. He swung her up into his arms and carried her up the stairs and out the front door. By the time he reached the median in front of the school, his lungs were screaming for oxygen and he collapsed to his knees in the snow. Daisy tumbled from his arms. He bent over, coughing again. But suddenly, she was on her knees in front of him, rubbing a palmful of snow across his face and another along the nape of his neck, coughing right along with him as she shocked his senses. "Are you with me? Harry, are you okay?"

He raised his head to meet her worried gaze. He hoped her eyes were irritated and watering, and that she wasn't wasting any tears on him. Still, he pulled off his heat-damaged glove and reached out with the pad of his thumb to wipe away the lines of moisture cutting tracks over her soot-stained cheek. "I'm okay."

"Don't lie to me." Even red-rimmed and weepy, that look over the top of her glasses wasn't one he could ignore.

"I'm okay *now*," he amended. Her skin was cool to the touch and she was shivering. "You're freezing." From the snow soaking through her jeans or the adrenaline leaving her system, it didn't matter. Harry pushed to his feet and peeled off his coat to wrap it around her shoulders. He hugged her to his chest and guided her to the cleared asphalt of the circular drive as a third fire engine pulled up.

A team of firefighters was already grabbing gear and fanning out around the building. A tall man in a white helmet was on his radio as he stepped down from the last truck. His slight limp didn't detract from the square set of his shoulders and air of authority. He was clearly the man in charge. After a brief chat with the principal and custodian, he sent one of his men off to cut the power to the building. Daisy huddled even closer against Harry when the chief approached them. "You're the teacher who called this in?"

"Yes. Daisy Gunderson."

Harry relished the cold night air seeping through his sweater and T-shirt because it kept his head clear, but he wished he had a little more body heat to share with Daisy. If she wasn't coughing, she was shaking, but he held her upright in one of those bear hugs she was so fond of. While she detailed the events and the chief deployed his crew into the building, Harry surveyed the parking lot through the swirl of emergency vehicle lights and first responders. The car with the yellow sticker was gone. Why hadn't he written down the license plate number? He hadn't even thought to look. Of course, the arsonist could have walked out the back door or had a car waiting for him someplace else. He was still no closer to identifying the creep terrorizing Daisy than he'd been when he'd first set up camp outside her home.

Harry snapped to when the crew chief addressed him. "She said you saw someone?"

Had he? "He was running up the east stairs, away from the fire. I didn't get a good look at him. That was five minutes before we got out of there."

"So, chances are he's clear of the scene and there's no one else inside. Can you describe him in case we run into him in there?"

Harry closed his eyes and replayed that brief impression distorted by heat and smoke. "Taller than me. Slender build." Shrugging, he opened his eyes. That was almost less than nothing to go on. "I can't even give you a hair color. I saw him from behind and he was wearing a blue coat and yellow hat."

Daisy lifted her chin. "Blue and gold? Like school colors?"

"Maybe. It was a blur."

"That narrows it down to about three-hundred people," she grumbled in a wheezing voice.

But the description seemed to be enough for the fire chief. "I'll go ahead and send a team in to sweep the building. Once we have the fire contained, we'll check the basement, too."

"He'll be long gone," Daisy added. "He thrives on me not knowing who he is."

"We'll check, all the same." He nodded toward the uniformed police officer waiting a few yards away. "The police will want to ask you the same questions."

Daisy nodded, but Harry felt her fingers curling into the front of his sweater. Her spirit might be willing, but her strength was flagging. "She needs a medic first. Probable smoke inhalation and shock."

"The ambulance is pulling up now." Harry and the chief walked her over to the ambulance where two EMTs sat Daisy in the back of the truck and immediately gave her oxygen and a blanket, and started taking her vitals. Before they made room for Harry to climb up, the tall firefighter tapped him on the shoulder. "Marine?" Harry nodded. The crew chief extended his hand. "John Murdock, USMC Retired. Did a couple of tours in Afghanistan."

Harry shook his hand, appreciating the bond that was always there between marines of any generation. "Master Sergeant Harry Lockhart. First Marine Expeditionary Force out of Pendleton. How did you know?"

"Not many men run *into* a fire except for firefighters and Devil Dogs." And maybe a crazy guy who thought he was about to lose someone he was learning to care about more and more with each passing minute. Before Harry could process exactly what that revelation meant, Murdock continued the conversation. "Lockhart. You any relation to Hope Lockhart Taylor?"

Harry nodded. "My sister."

Murdock nodded. "I thought something about you looked familiar. My boss, Meghan Taylor, is Hope's mother-in-law. I went to Hope and Pike's wedding a few years back." That had been the last time Harry had come home to Kansas City. He'd never realized how many people he was connected to beyond his sister here. "Small world, isn't it?"

"Bigger than I thought, actually."

Chief Murdock inclined his head toward the ambulance's interior. "Your friend hasn't taken her eyes off you. You'd better get in there and get checked out, too, so she stops worrying."

"Yes, sir."

Harry realized he shared another connection with John Murdock. As the older man limped away, he saw the distinctive void space of his pants catching around a steel rod above his boot. The KCFD crew chief had an artificial leg. They'd both sacrificed for their country. And apparently, John Murdock had adapted to civilian life just fine, even though all of him hadn't come home from the war, either.

Harry had never considered civilian life as an option for him. But if he did ever move on to life outside the Corps, he wanted it to be his choice—not because he was so broken that the Corps didn't want him. If he wasn't good enough for the USMC, how could he be good enough for anything, or anybody, else?

How could he be good enough for Daisy?

Forty minutes later, the fire was out and the building had been cleared. There was no sign of the man who'd set the blaze, unless his footprints were one of the hundreds tramped through the snow in the parking lot left by students and fans attending tonight's games or by the firefighters and police ensuring the entire school was secure. Harry sat on a gurney across from Daisy in the back of the ambulance as she sorted through her bag, making sure all her belongings—beyond the coat that obsessive creep had burned—were there. They reeked of smoke, and he couldn't detect that homey sweet scent that was uniquely hers anymore. He'd given his statement to the uniformed officer and a pair of detectives. He'd had his eyes rinsed, his vitals checked, and he'd held an oxygen mask over his nose and mouth for longer than he wanted, simply because Daisy took her mask down and asked him if he was all right every time he stopped the flow of purified air he wanted her to keep breathing. They were both wrapped in blankets, waiting to be cleared by the EMTs.

If he wasn't scaring her, then she was worried about him. He was raw with guilt. Hard to feel like much of a marine—like much of a man—when the only two emotions he could evoke from a pretty woman were fear and concern. He should reassess this unofficial mission. While he wasn't about to leave her alone against the jerk who wanted to hurt her, maybe he needed to rethink his whole plan to have Angel Daisy help him heal. She didn't need his kind of mess in her life.

"Harry?" He must have been quiet for too long because Daisy was sliding across the ambulance to sit on the gurney beside him. She tucked her hands beneath his arm and leaned her head against his shoulder. "Talk to me. We've been long-distance friends for a long time, and I know I don't have any real claim on you. Still, it's crazy how fast I've gotten used to having you around. But for a few seconds down there in the basement, I thought you'd left me."

He adjusted his blanket around both of them and rested his cheek against the crown of her head. Dr. Polk had advised him that the first step in dealing with his problem was admitting the extent of it.

"For a few seconds there, I did."

Chapter Eight

Harry got up to pace the house again.

The first two times he'd come downstairs from the guest room, the dogs had trotted out from Daisy's bedroom to inspect the noise and identify his presence. The two little dogs had trotted back into her room to go back to sleep. Caliban limped around the house with him, reminding Harry of the hundreds of night patrols he and Tango had gone on together. It was a bittersweet treat to work with a well-trained dog again. Caliban was willing to answer his commands to go out ahead of him and come back, to seek, to sit and to play a game of tug-of-war with his rope toy before the older dog, too, tired and went back to his comfy spot in Daisy's bedroom.

Losing a leg hadn't stopped the retired K-9 officer from belonging somewhere and having a purpose. Just because Caliban wasn't serving KCPD anymore didn't mean he didn't have a home and companions and a reason to get up in the morning—or the middle of the night when restless house guests roamed the halls and raided the cookie supply in the kitchen.

There was a lesson to be learned there. But the hour was late and a lot of the things Harry was feeling since first ringing Daisy's doorbell were new and alien to him.

The dogs must be getting used to the sound of his tread on the floors because none of them came out to greet him this time. Good. He hoped they stayed close to their mistress and that all of them were getting a good night's sleep. Daisy had stayed up far too late, running their clothes through the laundry twice, to rid them of the smells of smoke and acetone. Pike had brought over Harry's duffel bag with all his belongings and stayed to keep watch on the house while Harry showered the grime and nightmares off his skin. Then Daisy had soaked in the tub for nearly an hour before declaring she finally felt tired enough to sleep and had gone to bed.

Harry came down the stairs in his jeans and bare feet, with his M9 strapped to his hip. The enemy was different and the temps were colder, but this detail wasn't different from any other watch he'd served over the years. There was somebody out there who wanted to hurt the thing he'd sworn to protect. He stopped at the window beside the front door, folded his arms over his bare chest and stared out into the moonless night. Although the snow on the ground reflected the glow of the street lights, there were plenty of shadows, plus darkened vehicles and shaded windows in other homes where someone could hide. Still, the neighborhood looked secure for the moment. Unlike all the activity at Daisy's school earlier that night, this part of Kansas City seemed quiet.

Didn't make it any easier for him to fall asleep.

But he'd be damned if he'd get hooked on those sleeping pills Lt. Col. Biro said he would prescribe for him.

Harry could get by with an occasional nap and dozing on and off through the night. Maybe staring at something besides the tin-tiled ceiling in the upstairs guest room would be enough of a change of pace for him to grab some much needed rest. He'd give one of the recliners in Daisy's living room a try. At least on the ground floor, he'd be closer to any ingresses an intruder might use to break in. Surely, that was enough of an advantage to drop the alert buzzing through his veins to a level that would allow him thirty winks.

After checking the mudroom door and backyard, Harry wandered into the kitchen. He poured himself a glass of milk and downed half of it before eyeing the cookie jar again. One more reindeer cookie would take the edge off his growly stomach and give his taste buds something to savor instead of focusing every brain cell on replaying nightmares and envisioning the stalker he wanted to take down with his bare hands. He hoped the cookies weren't all for that party Daisy kept talking about, because he'd made a serious dent in her supply. He'd have to buy her some groceries or run to the bakery for her, although he had a feeling store-bought cookies wouldn't taste as good.

He was licking the icing off his fingertips when he strolled into the living room and found Daisy standing there in front of the empty fireplace, staring at him. His hands went instinctively to his shoulder and chest to cover himself, not out of modesty, but out of horror that she was getting a full-on view of the scarring he hid from the rest of the world. He couldn't hide his face, but why the hell hadn't he taken two seconds to put on a T-shirt?

He was glad that the only light in the room seeped in from the night-light in the kitchen and the glow from a street lamp filtering through the sheer curtains at the front door. "Have a nightmare?"

"I was worried about you, beating yourself up because you don't think you did a good enough job protecting me. The way I see it, the alternative is that I would have suffocated from the smoke and fumes if you hadn't been there."

Daisy crossed the room and reached for his hands, lacing their fingers together and holding on as she pulled them away from his disfigurement. He held himself still as she studied the hard ridges, stitch marks and skin grafts that were pinker and lighter than the rest of his chest, wishing he could spare her the horrific events that she must be imagining. She tilted her gaze above the brown glasses—that were far too plain for her colorful style—up to his for a moment before she released his hands and walked straight into his chest. She wound her arms around his waist and turned her cheek against the very scars he thought would repulse her. Her breasts pillowed against him, and the undamaged half of him was awkwardly aware of the tender nipples pearling against him. When her damp hair caught beneath his chin and her lips grazed across his collarbone, Harry surrendered to their mutual need to be held, and wound his arms around her back.

Daisy squeezed him in a hug, and Harry automatically tightened his hold on her, pulling her onto her toes. "Yes, I had a nightmare. About what happened tonight, and I was wondering if we could talk?"

Her voice trailed away, allowing him a glimpse of the vulnerability she worked far too hard to hide. He nuzzled the crown of her head, unsure that comfort was the best thing he could give her. From this angle, he could see the damp tendrils of purple and brown clinging to the collar of her flannel pajamas. And heaven help him, he could see and feel the siren silhouette of her hourglass figure cinched in at the waist by her robe. As much as he wanted to hide his own body, he wanted to see more of hers. He imagined everything about her was soft and touchable— from that shampooed hair to those sweet lips and delectable curves, right on down to the fuzzy green socks that covered her toes.

An answering male heat licked through his veins, reminding Harry that at least one part of him hadn't been affected by nightmares or injury. Everything about Daisy being here, standing close enough for him to breathe her scent, reminded him of how much time had passed since he'd been with a woman, how badly he needed a woman's gentle touch. But he reined in that feverish blast of longing that was stirring where her thighs pressed against his—this woman only wanted to talk.

"What's up?" he asked, mentally beating back his hormones and focusing on her needs, not his. He moved his grip to her shoulders and urged her warm body away from him.

Her gaze had landed on the gun he wore. "Do you sleep with that?" Before he could answer, her gaze bopped up to his. "Or don't you sleep at all?"

"I don't wear it *in* bed if that's what you mean. But I keep it close." Harry released her to unhook his belt and remove the Beretta and its holster. He set the weapon up on the mantel. "I don't want to be too far from our best protection. But I don't want to scare you more than I already do." He gestured toward the pair of recliners facing the fireplace. Separate seats would be best, considering the ill-timed lust simmering in his veins. "Shall we?"

"You don't scare me, Harry. I'm not afraid for me, at any rate." Once she settled in the first recliner, Harry sat in the other. But before he could raise the footrest, Daisy surprised him by moving over to his chair and sitting in his lap. "Is this okay? I want you to be comfortable. I have a feeling you won't like what I need to talk about."

He had a feeling he wouldn't, either. She wanted to finish that conversation they'd started during the game. For some reason he couldn't yet comprehend, Daisy was feeling the same attraction he was, but she wanted to know just how screwed up he was before anything else happened between them.

And yet, she was sitting in his lap, her hand braced at the center of his chest. Her hip and bottom warmed his thighs and…other things. "After everything that happened, you want to be with me?"

Her fingertips clenched into his skin. "Do I scare *you*?"

"A little. But I'm not saying no." Harry raised the footrest and leaned back, pulling Daisy into his arms and letting her settle into the chair, half beside and half on top of him, giving his body a taste of her curves pressed against him. He curled his right arm around her back, his hand hovering above her before settling on the swell of her hip in a grip that felt more possessive than it should. Her body was as perfect a fit as he'd imagined it would be, and that desire he'd tried to check flared to life again. But she needed to talk, and maybe he did, too. With his left hand, he sifted his fingers into her hair, smoothing damp strands off her face, stirring her sweet scent around him. "I should have stuck closer to you tonight, and not let everything get to me."

When her glasses butted against his chest, and got pushed askew, he took them off and lay them on the table beside them. She snuggled into a more comfortable position, brushing her stockinged feet against his bare toes and tucking her forehead at the juncture of his neck and shoulder. He was okay with her not being able to see him clearly. Talking about his past was going to be hard enough without Daisy seeing how ill-equipped he was to handle this kind of emotional intimacy.

"I don't blame you for what happened, Harry."

"I blame myself."

"You have post-traumatic stress. I remember when I was in the hospital after Brock's attack, I was so afraid of men that I only wanted female doctors and nurses working on me. Then Mom told me my father had died. She blamed me for bringing Brock into our lives and causing Dad so much stress. I blamed myself." Where was she going with this? When he felt her tensing against him, Harry covered her hand where it rested against his chest, silently telling her it was okay to continue. "I curled up into a ball in that hospital bed and wanted to be left completely alone. I didn't want anyone touching me, talking to me. I holed up in this house once I was released. I didn't see anyone but my lawyer. I didn't do anything but help Mom go through Dad's things and sleep."

"You? You're the most social creature I've ever met."

She switched the position of their hands, lacing her fingers with his. "PTSD. I was depressed. I got counseling. I made it through Brock's trial and Mom remarrying and moving away. And then, finally, one day I was done with it. I didn't want to be sad and paranoid anymore. I didn't want the bad guys—the bad feelings—to control my life. I got busy living again. Got a new teaching position. Got Muffy from her elderly owner who was moving into a nursing home and rescued Patch from the shelter. I started fixing up this house. I wanted to do for others and make friends and have a meaningful life."

"You've succeeded."

"But I needed that time to heal. So do you. Losing Tango must have devastated you." He tightened his grip around hers, confirming her suspicion. "I know you've lost friends. You nearly lost your own life. Be kind to yourself. Be patient. I believe you'll eventually learn to cope, too."

"I don't know. I was almost out of control tonight."

"Almost. So you yelled. To my way of thinking, you were yelling for help." She tilted her face away from his neck and cupped his damaged jaw, asking him to meet her solemn gaze. "You didn't hurt me. Trust me, I know what it's like to be hurt."

Harry touched his lips to hers for a brief kiss, sitting up enough to slide his hand behind the crook of her knees, pulling her across his lap so he could hold more of her in his arms. "I hate that you know that."

"The smells of the fire were a powerful trigger for your flashback. I imagine someone coming at me with a knife would do the same for me. In the meantime, I do the best I can every day. I try to be honest about what I'm thinking and feeling, but I try to stay positive and keep moving forward." She wiggled in his grasp, innocently planting her hip against his groin and snuggling beneath his chin again. "And I give myself a break when I don't. You should try it."

The tension in him eased at the gentle reprimand.

"How do I express what I'm thinking and feeling without completely losing it?"

She traced mindless circles across his chest and shoulder as she considered her answer. "What would you say if you were writing it to me in a letter?"

He was aware of each surviving nerve ending waiting in hopeful anticipation for her fingers to brush across it again. "Dr. Polk suggested something similar—that I start journaling. Write things down and get 'em out of my head so I'm not always fighting to control everything in there. But I wouldn't know where to start."

"Sure you do. Give me the rough draft. I'm an English teacher—I can make sense of just about anything. The beginning is usually the hardest part for my students. But you know how to start a letter."

"Dear Daisy?"

"So far, so good."

"I thought I was going to lose you tonight."

The circles stopped. "That's a dramatic opening."

"I'm not very good at jokes."

But she wasn't letting him off that easily. "The point is honesty, not humor. When you flashed back tonight, where did you go?"

His hand traveled up and down her back, squeezing her bottom and coming back to hug the nip of her waist before he mustered the courage to tell her about the insurgent sniper taking out Tango before the dog could pinpoint the two IEDs planted in an ambush. He told her about the two men he'd lost that day, including Albert Logan's pen pal, Benny Garcia.

He glossed over the details of shrapnel shredding his body and fire searing his face and neck. His speech was halting, his sentences disjointed. But with his senses focused on the scent of her hair and the heat of her sensuous body warming his, other defenses inside his head crumbled. He'd gotten what was left of Tango and his men out of there before blacking out. Then he didn't remember anything until waking up in the hospital in Germany.

He'd been angry. All the time. Afraid he might lose his eye or the use of his arm. He'd been wild with guilt—about the dog who'd been with him since Day One of shipping into the hot zone, and about the men he was responsible for who weren't coming home. He'd endured numerous surgeries and painful rehab. He'd been taken off active duty, told he wasn't good enough to do the job he loved anymore. He'd talked to shrinks—reawakened memories of the violence from his childhood, felt that same violence seething inside him and had been afraid he couldn't control it. He'd read Daisy's letters, over and over, clinging to the hope in her words, internalizing the wisdom and compassion she'd shared.

When he made it back to the present, Harry realized his skin was wet and that Daisy was trembling against him. He cupped her chin and tipped her face up to his, inspecting the pain he'd inflicted there. "Damn it, I'm making you cry again."

"That means I'm not just hearing, I'm feeling what you're saying." Bracing her hands on his shoulders, she closed the few inches separating them to press a kiss to his lips. When he responded, she lingered, and the quiet kiss lasted for several endless moments. Her tongue reached out to his in a tentative mating dance and Harry caught it, caressed it, before thrusting his tongue into her mouth and continuing the dance there. Harry felt the tender solace all the way down to his toes before he tasted the salt of her tears on her lips and he pulled away.

"Daisy—"

"Stop it. If you can yell, I can cry." She slid a hand behind his neck, scraping her palm over the short cut of his hair. "It's an honest expression of emotion. You should try it sometime."

Harry anchored his hands at her waist, keeping her from moving close enough to resume the kiss. "You want honest? When I lost it tonight in that fire, you were afraid of me." She squinted, keeping him in focus, listening to his words as she always had. "I never want to see that look in your eyes again. What if something happens and I scare you?"

"What if it doesn't? What if I cry again? Are you going to stop caring?"

She knew he had feelings for her? "No."

"Then why do you think *I* would?" She stroked the back of his neck, sending soothing comfort and tremors of anticipation down his spine and out to every working nerve in his body. "Crap happens to people sometimes. You get help, you work through it—you do the best you can. Sometimes you falter, but you get up and try again—and with the important people in your life, that's all that really matters."

His arms shook, the whole chair vibrating with the tension and doubt working through him. "You've never been afraid of me, have you? Even beat up and scarred like I am, you hug like it's going out of style. You kiss, you grab, you talk—"

"Sounds a little annoying when you put it that way."

He shook his head, still wrapping his mind around the idea that Daisy wanted to be with him. "I'm taking advantage of your kindness."

"You're giving me value by trusting me with your fears, by sharing your darkest feelings, by helping me understand you." She pushed a lock of hair out of her eyes and Harry's fingers were there to capture the silky wave and tuck it behind her ear. "I was with Brock for a year and a half. Believe me, I'll take trust and honesty with a fractured brain and sexy masculinity over control and isolation any day."

His fingers feathered into her hair. "Sexy?"

"Beautiful eyes, muscles for days." He held himself still as she crawled up his body. She gently kissed the lid above each eye, then kissed his cheek, the point of his chin, the hollow of his neck, gently, seductively working her way down to his chest where she kissed both the scarred surface and the healthy skin that leaped with eagerness at her touch. "Interesting that *sexy* is the word you keyed in on."

"After everything I've told you, you still want this—us—to happen?"

She harrumphed a dramatic sigh, folded her arms over his chest and rested her chin there. "I'm lying on top of you, I can feel your arousal pressing against my hip, which is really good for my ego because it means I'm halfway irresistible, and if you don't kiss me—I mean, really kiss me like I think you want to—soon, then I'm just going to keep right on talking. And you will never be able to shut me up."

"You aren't halfway anything." Harry didn't need much encouragement to give in to what his body had been craving.

He righted the chair, spilling Daisy into his lap. His hands were there to catch her bottom and pull her back against his chest. She slipped her arms around his neck, welcoming his kiss as he laid claim to her beautiful mouth. He wasn't smooth, but he was hungry for her. Her fingers teased the nape of his neck again, skidded over his prickly hair, then boldly framed his face to keep their lips aligned as her knees parted and dropped to either side of his thighs. Her warm soft heat cupped the aching desire growing stiff inside his jeans and he moaned. He needed more. He needed everything.

Harry moved his hands to the front of her robe to free the knot, knocking into her hands as they worked the top button of his jeans. She laughed and he pressed his lips to the sound in her throat. The angle was wrong, and he was a little too ready for her to work his zipper down, so he caught her wrists and moved her hands to his chest where they happily explored each spasm of muscle that yearned for her touch.

Harry pushed her robe open and tugged at the buttons of her pajama top. Flowered flannel shouldn't be so damn sexy, but it was as he dragged the soft cotton over her shoulders and down her arms, revealing her heavy breasts to his appreciative gaze. The tips were a pretty pink, and straining to attention in the chilly air.

Her arms were trapped in the ends of the sleeves, but he let her wiggle herself free. He was too busy sliding his hands around to the soft skin of her back while he dropped his lips to the generous swell of one breast, and then the other, catching a nipple in his mouth when it bounced too close. Harry closed his lips around the tip, laving the sweet bud with his tongue until he heard a whimper against his ear.

"I'm sorry." Harry withdrew immediately, drawing in deep breaths to reclaim his equilibrium. He clasped her face between his hands and sought out any sign of pain he might have caused in her darkened blue eyes. "I can't feel everything I do to you. There's nerve damage. If I'm doing something you don't like—"

"That, sir, was the brink of ecstasy. I'll let you know when I'm not enjoying myself." Daisy freed her arms from the sleeves that bound her, cupped either side of his jaw and guided his mouth to the other breast.

She didn't say another word.

Harry scooped Daisy up in his arms and carried her to her bedroom. After scooting the dogs out and closing the door, he pulled out his wallet and tossed it onto the bedside table before shucking his jeans and shorts and climbing onto the bed beside her.

Daisy had stripped off her pajama bottoms and was reaching for him. But he pushed her back into the pillows, wanting to feast his eyes first. In the soft glow of the bedside lamp, he took in every inch of her. She was too much, too beautiful…too vulnerable. His gaze stopped on the small pucker of scar tissue on the underside of her breast. He gently touched the tip of his finger to it. He wasn't the only wounded warrior here.

Harry leaned over to kiss the permanent evidence of the brutal attack she'd survived. She flinched and tried to roll away, but he wouldn't let her. "You've seen me."

After she lay back against the pillows, baring herself completely to him, he reverently touched each scar, first with his hand and then with his lips. He kissed her chest, her belly, her breasts, until her hands were on his hair again, holding his mouth to each mark as if his touch healed her the way she was healing him.

He lingered over one mark just below her belly button, his heated breath raising goose bumps over her quivering flesh. "Are you…okay…inside? Did he…?"

"The surgeon removed my spleen and one ovary and the Fallopian tube, and he sewed up a nick in one of my lungs and my stomach. Theoretically, I can still make babies, so we need to use protection." He lifted his head to meet her squinting gaze. "Otherwise, what you see is what you get."

"I want it." Harry climbed over her the way she had climbed up his body in the chair, and claimed her mouth for a deep, drugging kiss. "I want you."

"Please tell me you have something in that wallet."

Harry rolled off her to retrieve the foil packet from the bedside table. "It's dusty, but it should be reliable."

He felt a kiss between his shoulder blades as he sat on the edge of the bed and sheathed himself. "Dust it off, Marine. You have a job to do."

Do this.

It was the most glorious order he'd ever obeyed.

Daisy climbed onto his lap before he'd even considered a position. But he was just fine with this one. Stars exploded behind his eyes as she sank, wet and hot and ready, over his shaft. Oh, yeah, he was more than fine with this position. Already matching her rhythm and rocking inside her, he kissed her breasts, nibbled her neck, claimed her lips until the need became too great. Harry squeezed her in a tight hug, clamping every curve of her body against his as he detonated inside her.

Daisy cried out with her release and Harry held her to him until the waves of her climax faded away and her head collapsed against his neck. They fell back onto the bed together, with Daisy resting on top of him for several long minutes until their breathing returned to normal and the perspiration on their bodies began to cool.

Then Harry tucked her under the covers and made a quick trip to the bathroom to dispose of the condom. Daisy was half asleep when he returned, but she was smiling as he crawled under the quilts with her and gathered her into his arms.

She wedged one soft thigh between his and wrapped her arm around his waist, clinging to him in a very sexy version of a hug. Harry stroked his fingers up and down her back, feeling a rare, satisfied fatigue creeping into his muscles. He couldn't believe that any man would try to control this woman's brave spirit and generous heart. She was such a gift.

Such a completely unexpected gift. This Daisy wasn't anything like the woman in his letters.

Harry's fingers came to rest beneath her soft, damp hair. "For some reason, from your letters, I pictured you as a blonde."

"I was once." That made him laugh and he felt her smile against his skin. "You have a wonderful laugh. You should practice it more often."

He'd never had much reason to. "I will if you don't change your shampoo."

Don't change anything about you.

"Strange request." She yawned and burrowed in beside him.

Harry drifted off to sleep along with her, his nose buried in the sweet scent of her hair. No stranger than Harry Lockhart falling in love with her all over again.

This time, with the real Daisy Gunderson.

DAISY WAS IN a deep, blank sleep when she startled awake to a man's hand clamped over her mouth.

Her muffled scream quickly fell silent when Harry's face hovered into focus above hers. He pressed a finger to his lips and didn't remove his hand until she nodded her understanding to remain quiet. Her clock was a blur of red light from this distance, leaving her adrift with no idea of the time or situation. The sun wasn't even up yet. But sometime in the hours since that cathartic conversation and making love, while she was replete with satisfaction and feeling more cherished than she had with any man in her life, Harry had been getting dressed and sneaking around the house.

Well, half-dressed. As far as she was concerned, the man never needed to put on a shirt again. Not that that was terribly practical, but Harry's fit, supple body moving over to the window and back to the edge of her bed certainly improved the scenery.

"Dais?" he whispered. "Honey, are you awake?"

Honey? Focus!

Something was wrong. Even in her nearsighted haze, she could see Harry was strapping on his gun again. She pulled the sheet around her and sat up as he handed her the brown glasses they'd left in the living room.

She slipped them on, hoping that bringing clarity to his grim expression would give her understanding. "What is it?" She heard one of the dogs growling from the foot of the bed, and all the beautiful aftermath of making love vanished in a clutch of fear. "Harry?

He pushed her phone into her hands. "Call 9-1-1. There's someone outside."

That's when Daisy jumped at the pop, pop, pop of tiny explosions and shattering glass out on the back deck. Muffy leaped onto the corner of the bed and barked an alarm. Patch jumped up beside him, yapping with equal fury. Harry swore at the noisy outburst.

Those pops hadn't been gunshots. But they definitely weren't anything natural. Neither was the distinct sound of running footsteps.

Harry was already moving to her bedroom door, drawing his gun. The man wasn't prepped for battle. He didn't even have shoes on. "You can't—"

There was no pretense of hushed and discreet now.

"Get dressed. Stay in this room. I'm leaving the dogs in here with you. Caliban, *Pas Auf.*" Apparently, that meant he should guard the place because the Belgian Malinois never moved from his post, even after Harry pulled the door shut.

Daisy slipped out of bed, pulled on her jeans and the first top she could find and placed the call.

Chapter Nine

At the swirl of red and white lights pulling up in front of the house, Daisy zipped up Harry's coat and ran to the mudroom door, eager to see where Harry had gone when he'd run out the back. Had he found the man who'd been terrorizing her? Or—the frightening possibility entered her head before she could stop it—had the man found Harry?

She unlocked the door and dashed onto the deck. "Harry?"

Her boot crunched with the first step, then the second, and she stopped. She was walking on glass. The security light had been shattered and she was walking across dozens of broken Christmas light bulbs. The path of so much destruction littering her deck and the sidewalk down to the gate was disturbing enough.

The little dots of blood that grew into half a bloody footprint triggered a different kind of fear. "Harry!"

Without the lights, the air was dim, but with the sun cresting the horizon in the east, the trail of bloody prints through the snow was easy to follow. There were two sets of footprints now, far apart, left by one man running after the other. "Harry?"

Daisy broke into a run. Harry was hurt. Protecting her, he'd gotten hurt.

"Harr—" She spotted his back and the legs of his quarry when she reached the front of the house…the same time she saw the two uniformed officers duck behind the open doors of their cruiser and pull their guns, ordering Harry to stand down. Daisy ran toward the cops, her hands raised in a plea. "Officers, wait! Don't shoot!"

"Damn it, Daisy, I told you to stay inside," Harry warned. He was facing the house, his broad body blocking the man he had pinned to the siding. The tension radiating off his body was thicker than the wintry dampness hanging in the air. Tiny shards of colored glass littered the snow out here, too, and she looked up to see dangling wires and empty sockets where her Christmas decorations used to hang. There were indentations in the snow beside the porch where a scuffle must have occurred, but apparently, Harry had put an end to it. Although she couldn't see the man, she could hear him panting, almost blubbering with fear after losing a fight to Harry. "This guy busted up every one of your decorations. He's angry with you."

"I know. I saw it. One of you is bleeding," she added, hoping he might reassure her that he was in one piece and the other guy wasn't mortally wounded.

"I'm not letting him go. If he'd done that to you instead of a bunch of—"

"Gun!" one of the officers shouted.

Daisy moved closer to the police car, placing herself in the potential line of fire. The two men immediately lowered their weapons if not their guard. "I'm Daisy Gunderson. I called this in. This man is with me. There haven't been any gunshots. He caught the intruder I reported. My house has been vandalized, and he caught this guy running away. Don't hurt him."

The shorter of the two officers holstered his weapon while the other came around the hood of the cruiser to back him up. "I'm Officer Cho, KCPD. I'd feel a lot better if that weapon he's wearing was secured."

"What if I hand it over to you?" Daisy suggested.

Cho nodded. "Slow and easy."

"Harry?" Daisy announced herself before creeping up behind him. His skin was wet and ice-cold as she touched his back. "I'm going to hand your gun over to the officer so they can put their weapons away. I don't want anyone here to get hurt."

The ramrod tension she felt beneath her hand didn't waver. "Do it."

She unhooked the snap on his holster and moved in beside him to pull out the gun. Once she had the weapon safely in hand she looked up and gasped in surprise.

"Angelo?"

Harry had her prize student flattened against the

house. Stunned was an understatement for the shock chilling her from the inside out. The teenager was crying, but his eyes were clear as his gaze darted to hers.

"Ms. G.," he gasped. He pawed at Harry's forearm. Although his gold Central Prep ball cap had been knocked off his head and was crushed under his feet, he didn't appear to be harmed. Frightened, yes, but not hurt. "I wasn't thinking. Tell your boyfriend how sorry I am. I didn't mean it."

There was that boyfriend word again.

"Harry. Let him go. He's half your age. He doesn't know how to fight like you do." She handed the gun off to Officer Cho and came back to gently lay her hands on Harry's arm and shoulder. "He's just a kid."

"I've seen kids do worse. Decoys, suicide bombers."

"You're not in a war zone. You're in Kansas City. With me. And I'm safe. Look at me. I'm fine. KCPD is here now. Let them handle it. Angelo won't hurt me. Please let him go."

Harry shifted his gaze to hers. His eyes were shadowed, and that taut muscle ticked beneath his right eye. Then he nodded, stepped back and Angelo was free. "Sorry, kid."

"I did it," Angelo confessed, scurrying around Harry. The young man looked relieved to be dealing with the officer asking him about weapons, feeling his pockets and handcuffing him, rather than facing Harry Lockhart. "I broke all the lights. It was me."

Daisy's heart was crushed. She needed answers

for any of this to make sense. Why would Angelo want to do this to her? Why hadn't she known he was sending her those gifts? Why? There were other questions that needed answers, too. She pointed to the trail of blood in the snow. "Whose blood is that?"

"Not his." Harry lifted each foot from the snow. Her heart stuttered again when she saw several small cuts oozing blood on the pale skin of his feet.

"Why don't you go inside and finish getting dressed. There's a first-aid kit in the downstairs bathroom. Unless you need my help?"

"I don't need anybody's help." He looked down at her concerned expression and relented the argument. He scooped up Angelo's cap and placed it back on the young man's head before the officer walked him to the cruiser. "Did I hurt you, kid?"

Angelo's head shook with a jerk. "No, sir."

"You scared of me?"

"Yes, sir."

"Good. Then you know not to do anything that'll upset Ms. G. again, right?"

Angelo nodded.

Harry shifted his gaze to the two police officers, glancing down at the gun tucked into the shorter man's belt. "I'm an NCO with the US Marines, home on leave. My ID is inside the house, but I've got a permit to carry that thing. It hasn't been fired. I'll be back out in ten to give my statement and retrieve it."

Officer Cho identified himself in a way that Harry seemed to appreciate. "Captain. Missouri Army National Guard." The shorter man okayed Harry's departure with one condition. "Officer Bulkey here is going to accompany you."

"Yes, sir." Harry gave the officer a curt nod before the two men went inside the house.

Angelo took half a step toward Daisy before Cho tugged on his cuffs and warned him to keep his distance. "Sorry, Ms. G. I was just mad that you… That he…" He looked up at the house where Harry had disappeared before inhaling a deep breath and spewing out his confession. "You haven't had a boyfriend in all the time I've known you. And now GI Joe shows up for Christmas? In a month I'm going to be eighteen. Then those stupid rules at school don't apply. You and me, we've got a thing. I was going to ask you out."

"Angelo, I can't date you. Even if you are legal age. I wouldn't jeopardize my job or your school year. And we don't have a thing." Daisy sputtered, replaying the year and a half she'd had Angelo in junior and senior English, trying to think of what she might have said or done that would have given him the slightest hint of encouragement. "I've always enjoyed having you in class. Just because I believe in your talents and abilities doesn't mean I have those kinds of feelings for you."

"But I have those feelings for you." Angelo leaned toward her, his young face lined with hurt. "Then Albert said he saw you two making out."

That peck on the lips at the game? That was all Albert could have seen. Nothing else had happened between her and Harry until they'd gotten home.

How could one tentative kiss in a public place equate to so much anger and violence?

"Angelo, I could have died in that fire last night."

"What fire?"

He didn't know? She couldn't help but notice he matched the vague description of the man Harry had seen running from the blaze—blue team coat, gold hat. "In the school basement, after the game."

The teenager's brown eyes widened with concern. "Are you okay? Is the school still there? We've got a home tournament next Saturday."

More than her suspicion that he wasn't a very good liar, Angelo's sudden shift in loyalty to his true love—basketball—eased her fear that her student could be Secret Santa. The broken decorations were a temper tantrum, a child not getting his way and lashing out. Hormones. Crazy teenage hormones and a misplaced crush. Not some sick obsession that promised to hurt her. That was all this was, right? All the same, she had to ask, "Have you been sending me gifts?"

He shrugged, confused by the question. "I gave you Granny's caramels."

"No anonymous cards? Presents?"

"No, ma'am." His concern had moved away from her. "Did the school burn down?"

She almost laughed. Almost. "No. You'll still have to show up for class on Monday."

Officer Cho interrupted the conversation. "Ms. Gunderson, I'm going to read Angelo his rights and put him in the back of the cruiser. No sense us all standing out in the cold. Since you seem to know him, do you want to handle this or would you like to press charges?"

"Press charges?" Angelo gasped. "Oh, hell no. I'll get benched."

He'd probably only get probation if this incident ever made it in front of a judge, but that could cost his chance at a good scholarship. The teacher in Daisy took over for the woman who'd been so worried and afraid. She squeezed Angelo's arm, giving him her sternest teacher look. "You wait in the car with Officer Cho for now. Let me make a couple of phone calls to see if we can get this straightened out. But there will be consequences."

Officer Cho nodded, turning Angelo toward the police car.

"Don't call Granny," Angelo begged. "Please, Ms. G. She will tan my hide and I'll be hauling groceries and taking out trash for every old lady in my building for a month."

Although she wasn't a proponent of hide-tanning, the rest sounded like a fair trade-off. Daisy pulled her phone from the pocket of Harry's coat. She had another idea, a consequence that would mean something to Angelo without jeopardizing his future. "I'll see what I can do."

An hour later, the sun was shining on her front porch. The daylight sparkled off the ice crystals in the snow and warmed the air to a tolerable twenty degrees. Officers Cho and Bulkey had left to file their reports, and Angelo was sitting in the passenger seat of Bernie Riley's car, waiting for the basketball coach to drive him home. Coach Riley promised to have a heart-to-heart talk with his starting point guard about inappropriate crushes on English teachers, and how it was a bad idea to trash her Christmas decorations because he was jealous of the grown man paying attention to her.

Hopefully, Bernie would get started on that heart-to-heart soon. For now, the tall man was standing on Daisy's porch, ignoring her surly house guest leaning against the white pillar behind him, thanking her for not pressing charges against his star player. "I'll have him running extra laps and coming in early to practice his free throws. And I'll make sure he's back here this afternoon to clean up the mess he made," Bernie affirmed, as if the idea had been his and not hers. "I'll clear things with his grandmother, too. We'll make sure he knows he's done something wrong without involving the police and endangering his standing at school."

"I appreciate you coming over, Bernie."

"Not a problem. Always happy to help you out, Gunderson."

He leaned in to give her a hug that felt awkward, not just because of the faintly pungent smell clinging to his clothes that stung Daisy's nose, or the fact that she'd hugged him maybe once, at last year's Christmas party—but because she was blatantly aware of Harry's gray eyes drilling holes in the other man's back. At least he made no effort to *take him down* as he'd reported to the police when Angelo had run from him earlier.

When Bernie pulled away and started down the steps, Daisy breathed a sigh of relief. But she regretted the momentary celebration when Bernie stopped on the bottom step and turned to face her. "Hey. I heard about those gifts you've been getting from your Secret Santa. The naughty ones."

Naughty was a politically correct way to describe them, she supposed. Daisy hugged her arms around the front of Harry's coat. "After the fire, I guess word has spread all over the school."

"Pretty much." Bernie reached up under his gold stocking cap and scratched his head, frowning before he smoothed it back into place. "I think you should know that I'm your Secret Santa."

"What?" She gasped, instantly recoiling. "You're Secret Santa?"

This time, Harry pushed away from the post. When he started down the steps after Bernie, she grabbed his arm. Although Harry halted at her touch, she slid her hand down to his and waited for him to lace his fingers with hers before she trusted that he was clearly in the moment with her.

"Let's hear him out," Daisy suggested.

Harry might be willing to listen, but he wasn't about to step down from protecting her from a possible threat. Standing with his shoulder between her and Bernie, he did as she asked. "So talk."

Bernie's green eyes looked serious for a change, and his tone was surprisingly genuine. "I'm not the one giving you those things. Someone must be replacing my gifts. I put the envelopes in your mailbox and the gifts on your desk—but I told Stella to get you the things on your list. Chocolate. Gift cards for coffee. Ornaments."

Daisy slipped her other hand down to hold on to Harry's unwavering strength. "Your wife is giving me those gifts?"

"I don't have time to shop." Bernie shrugged. "I don't like to shop. So she does all that for me. Wraps them up, sticks in the fancy cards. All I do is deliver."

"Why would your wife do that?"

"I'm not saying she's sending you those things. I mean, Stella gets crazy sometimes, but I don't think she even knows what some of that stuff in the pictures is. I mean, it's porn, right? She's uh, she's a lady."

Daisy had a feeling any woman of any background would know exactly the kind of violence the images in those drawings depicted.

"How do you know what's in the pictures?" Harry asked.

"Bosch and Gamblin were talking about it at the game last night."

"Eddie and Mary told you?" Her friends had betrayed her confidence?

"I could tell there was something funky going on with the present you got yesterday. I thought Stella might be trying to make me look bad by giving you a lump of coal." She should be so lucky. "I didn't know there was something wrong with the gifts until I saw what happened in the school basement. I was down there this morning after going over game tapes in my office. You must have been terrified. This morning I asked some people what was going on."

"Some people?"

"I called Principal Hague and he explained what was going on. Now that announcement he made at the faculty meeting about appropriate gifts makes sense." Bernie scratched under his cap again.

She felt the muscles in Harry's arm tense a split second before it snaked out and he snatched the gold stocking cap off Bernie's head.

"What the hell, dude?"

"You got a bad case of dandruff? Why do you keep scratching?" Harry put the cap up to his nose and instantly averted his face. "It smells like smoke and acetone."

Bernie snatched the cap back and pulled it over his head. "I told you I was down in the basement this morning. The place still reeks. Hague said they're airing out the whole school all weekend so we can get back in there on Monday."

Daisy supposed that was a perfectly logical explanation for a man with a blue jacket and yellow hat—like the man Harry had seen running from the fire—to have clothes that smelled like the crime scene. Although logic wasn't making it any easier to tamp down her suspicions about her colleague. "Where were you last night?"

"Coaching two ball games."

Harry took a step closer. "What about afterward? When did you leave? With the players? Later than that?"

Bernie puffed up to his six and a half feet of height. "Are you accusing me of something?" He sidled closer to Daisy, and Harry shifted, keeping his shoulder and dark-eyed glare between them. "Look, I came here to help you out, not to be given the third degree by your bully boyfriend here."

"Where were you?" Harry pressed. Had the smell of the cap triggered a bad memory? Was he getting angry again?

"None of your damn business." Bernie looked straight at Daisy, ignoring Harry. "I just wanted you to know that I drew your name for Secret Santa, and that Stella has been buying the gifts. She has high-class taste. I'm sure she's only getting you nice stuff. I don't know how they're getting swapped out for those other things or who's doing it. But I didn't want you to blame me. Or her." His forehead wrinkled with a rueful expression. "She and I—we've been having some troubles lately. Heck, I even thought about taking you up on renting that spare room of yours for a few weeks instead of staying in a hotel."

"A hotel?" Daisy knew she should feel sorry for Bernie instead of thinking that a struggling marriage could be a motive for either one of them to threaten her.

"Like I said, troubles. That room wouldn't still be available, would it? I've been keeping a change of clothes on me and showering at the school locker room in the morning. It'd be nice to be in a house again."

"She has a tenant," Harry announced. He draped his arm over her shoulders and squeezed her to his side, warning Bernie that no other man was going to get close to her while he was around.

A twinge of discomfort pinged in Daisy's memories and she quietly extricated herself from Harry's grasp. Had being protective of her just taken a step over the line into Brock Jantzen land?

Bernie got the message loud and clear, instantly backing off from the possibility of moving in with her. "Yeah. Well, if I had known the kind of stuff you were getting, I'd have said something sooner."

Daisy nodded, putting another step between her and Harry. "Thanks for letting me know."

Perhaps Bernie still didn't realize the depth of terror she'd been living with the past two weeks. "Guess that's going to ruin the party for you next Saturday. It won't be a surprise for you when we reveal who had whose name."

She'd already had plenty of surprises this week. She glanced over at the back of Harry's dark, close-cropped hair that she'd had such fun tickling her palms against last night. Only one of those surprises had been good. Harry Lockhart. The surprise of this relationship—if that was what it even was—was awkward. Difficult and uncertain. But a good surprise, nonetheless.

Cognizant of their audience here and in the car,

Daisy tabled her analysis over what, exactly, Harry meant to her, and whether the reality of a relationship with a man struggling with PTSD was something she wanted to take on. She waved to Angelo and offered Bernie a smile. "Thanks for helping with Angelo. And I'm sorry to hear about you and Stella."

"Thanks."

"Talk to her," Daisy suggested. "Listen, too. If you can communicate, you can solve just about anything." She wondered if Harry was hearing any of that advice. "And—maybe you shouldn't give me any more presents. Not even the big one for the party. Return it. Donate it to charity. Give it to someone else. If this guy doesn't have that anonymous way to send me gifts, maybe he'll stop."

"If you say so." Bernie strode around the clear path of the sidewalk and climbed into his car, doffing her a salute before driving away.

Harry watched the car all the way to the stop sign at the corner before looking up at her. "He won't stop."

Although she was the one wearing the coat, Daisy shivered and turned to the front door. "Thank you for those fine words of comfort."

He caught her hand and stopped her. "This isn't a joke. Perverts like that, they'll find a way to get to you if that's what they want. If you cut him off, if he thinks you're on to him, he might escalate."

"Someone locked me in a room and started a fire that could have killed me." So much for subtle hints. Daisy tugged her hand free, regretting that she'd forgotten the soldier sorely lacking verbal communication skills after being with the passionate, bravely vulnerable man last night. "Things have already escalated."

"Damn it, Daisy, I'm not making light of what happened." When she snatched her hand from his, he fell back to the top step. "Don't be a fool. What if Riley confessed to being your Secret Santa just to throw you off track so you wouldn't suspect him? Why do his clothes smell like that fire? What if Angelo isn't as innocent as you seem to think?"

"What if Stella Riley is so jealous of something she thinks I've done that she wants to torment me?" Daisy crossed the porch to look him straight in the eye. "I'm not stupid. You don't think I've thought of any of that? All I have are suspects and threats. What I don't have are answers. I don't know who to trust anymore. This isn't over. Not until I know who is doing this to me, and that creep is in jail. But I am—"

"—going to stay positive?" That was sarcasm, deriding her for the very trait he'd praised the night before.

"I was going to say I'm keeping my guard up."

"You didn't with me." He threw his hands up. "You worry too much about everybody else. You're too forgiving. You're going to get hurt."

"You're being a jerk right now, you know that?" The differences between them had finally erupted into an argument that neither one of them could win. His heart might be in the right place, believing he was protecting her, but she couldn't live her life being judged and criticized and ordered around. "Where's my Harry? Where's the man from those letters?"

He jolted back, as if she'd slapped him across the face. When he spoke again, it was a quiet, unemotional tone. "I warned you I wasn't any good at this. I was a different man then."

Daisy touched his chest, splaying her fingers until she could feel the strong beat of his heart beneath her hand. Her tone was hushed, too. "No. You're the same man. That's the man who was with me last night. But you went through something awful, more than a good man should have to bear. You just have to find him again."

That muscle ticked beneath his eye again as he evaluated her words. "You don't have to welcome me into your bedroom anymore, but I'm not leaving you unprotected. My gear's already upstairs. I'll sleep up there and start paying you rent."

He was serious about becoming her tenant, about taking a relationship that had heated to incendiary in the span of forty-eight hours back to let's-just-be-friends. Her life was safer this way, right? Her heart most certainly was. She should be glad that one of them could think sensibly here. Instead, she felt hollow inside, as though she'd lost something that was more important than she realized. "If that's how you want it."

"That's how it needs to be."

The man needed his distance. He didn't trust himself not to hurt her. But how was she ever going to accept that the man she'd fallen in love with didn't want to be in a relationship? He didn't believe he could be. "Harry—"

The dogs started barking inside the house, ending the conversation. All three of her fur-babies were at the storm door, telling her she had company. She recognized the bark. It was the I-spy-another-dog alert. Her neighbor, Jeremiah Finch, was strolling by with his Chihuahua, Suzy, on a long black leash. "Good morning, Daisy."

"Good morning, Mr. Finch." Harry didn't turn, didn't offer any polite greeting to the older man in his trim wool coat and neatly tied scarf. Harry snapped his fingers and used a hand signal to calm Caliban and Patch into a tail-wagging sit, leaving Muffy as the only noisemaker announcing their visitor. When Jeremiah stopped to let Suzy sniff out the new smells of all the visitors Daisy had had that morning, she moved off the porch to continue the conversation. "It's shaping up to be the nicest day we've had in weeks. I'm glad you and Suzy are getting out."

"I'm not sure I want to, even in the daylight."

"What do you mean?"

He clucked his tongue behind his teeth. "We have a crime wave in our neighborhood."

"A crime wave? You mean the police car that was here earlier?" She summoned a smile to reassure him that whatever was happening was only happening to her. "The situation has been taken care of."

"Has it?" He came halfway up her front walk, as if she couldn't hear him tsk-tsking over the short distance already. "Some punk vandalized your house.

I have trespassers in my backyard—one of my box-wood bushes was trampled on." He peeked around her, eyeing the gun strapped to Harry's thigh. "Men with guns are roaming at will—"

"Harry is not roaming the neighborhood."

Suddenly, Harry was interested in joining the con-versation. He trotted down the steps to join her, hold-ing up his phone. "Mr. Finch, do you mind if I take pictures of the footprints in your backyard?"

Jeremiah seemed taken aback to be addressed di-rectly by the bigger man. "As long as that's all you do."

With a nod, Harry jogged through the snow and disappeared around the corner of the house.

Once Harry was gone, Jeremiah tugged on Suzy's leash so he could lean in toward Daisy. "Don't think I didn't see your thug sitting outside your house the night before last. He was probably casing the joint. He's casing mine now. But I could hardly stop him. And you've invited him into your home. After what happened with your last boyfriend, I would think you'd be more careful about who you associate with. I try to keep an eye on you and protect you—"

"First of all, Master Sergeant Harry Lockhart is no thug. He's a decorated marine. Second, my stu-dent may be a misguided young man, but he is not a punk and he is no threat to you. If he damaged one of your bushes, I'll make sure he pays to replace it. And third, what happened to me is my business, not yours. How I protect myself is none of your concern."

"I can see you're upset." Jeremiah's face had

turned red all the way up to his hairline. "So, this person—is a bodyguard? What kind of threat are we talking about?" He clutched at his chest. "Am I in danger?"

"No." Daisy reached down to pet Suzy when the tiny dog put her paws on Daisy's knee. Dogs had always been a stress reducer for her. She couldn't imagine losing any one of hers the way Harry had lost Tango. "I'm sorry I lost my temper. I've been receiving threats. Harry is a…friend…who's helping me keep an eye on things."

"I see." Jeremiah tugged the Chihuahua back to his side. "I still don't like seeing guns in my neighborhood. And your friend is so…rough-looking. Are you certain you're safe with him?"

Wasn't that the question of the hour?

"I know you were friends with Mom and Dad, and you have been friends with me—but to come over to my home and lecture me about my choices…" Even if they were bad ones, he had no right to make her feel stupid for trusting her heart or wanting to help a good man. Mr. Finch didn't have that right. Harry didn't. No one did.

Jeremiah glanced over to the side yard where Harry had gone. "Well, if something happens and you do need me, you have my number. Come along, Suzy."

As Mr. Finch and Suzy moved on down the street to continue their walk, Daisy pressed her hands over her mouth, fighting back the urge to cry or cuss up a blue streak. She wouldn't apologize for defending the people she cared about, but there had to be a better way to cope with the fear and uncertainty and raging need to have control over her own life again. Maybe this was what Harry felt like when he lost it. But she was years past her trauma while his was still fresh. The stress was getting to be too much. She was tired of being afraid, of suspecting everyone she knew. She needed this to be done.

"Daisy?" She started at the clipped voice behind her, and quickly swiped at the tears in her eyes before they could fall. "Are you all right?"

She turned to face Harry, wishing she had the right to walk into his arms and be held. But there was a tension between them now that hadn't been there before, an underlying sizzle of attraction that was complicated in a big way by far too many issues that neither of them could control.

When she didn't answer, he pulled out his phone. "I found something important. Something that should exonerate Angelo."

"I never believed he was sending me those gifts."

"But would it make you feel better to know for sure? To have one less person around you who could be a suspect?"

He was trying to make her feel better? That earned him the shadow of a smile. He wasn't offering comforting words or a hug. But it would be nice to be able to look over her classroom on Monday and not have to be afraid of anyone there. "What did you find?"

"The footprints were made by two different kinds

of shoes. Angelo's has a tread, like a running shoe. The prints in Finch's yard, like the ones by your window the other night, were made by boots."

She wasn't comforted yet. "Maybe Angelo wore boots the other night to peek in my window. He's not so poor that he can't afford more than one pair of shoes."

"Only if he figured out a way to shrink his feet." Harry pulled up the pictures on his phone and showed her the images. "It's not scientific, but it's enough to make me suspicious." Harry had photographed all three sets of prints frozen in the snow, using his own boot as a marker beside each one to compare the size. Angelo's running shoes were a good two to three sizes bigger, while the others were smaller and skinnier than Harry's foot. "I'm going to send the pictures to Pike. He's not a detective, but he'll know who to show them to."

"Thank you." Daisy appreciated the effort he was making to ease some of her fear. Maybe it was the only way he thought he could help.

"I'm sorry I thought the worst of that kid. But it does prove that this guy isn't just targeting you at school. He knows where you live. He's been here. Watching you."

"And the gloom and doom is back." Daisy marched up the stairs into the house. She shooed the dogs ahead of her while Harry locked the door behind her. "You think I don't know that he's watching? That I don't feel him around me all the time?" Harry followed her into the kitchen where she poured herself a cup of coffee and held the steaming mug between her hands. "This is where you're supposed to say something to make me feel better."

When he didn't say anything, she shrugged out of his coat and tossed it at him. He dropped the coat onto a chair and followed her to the refrigerator. "I heard you defending me against Finch. You didn't have to do that. I was losing it with that kid. I got territorial with Coach Riley. I was making decisions without asking you. I'm fighting to keep you safe. But the way I talked to you—the words, the tone? I could tell I hurt you. Last night was…amazing. A perfect moment out of time between all the nightmares." Just as she closed her eyes to let the raw poetry of his words warm her battered heart, he added, "But I'm not good for you, Daisy. Maybe I am a thug."

She refused to believe that.

"Normal people have arguments just like we did. Normal people lose it every now and then. You're not going to be cured after one late-night conversation and…" *a perfect moment out of time.* Hugging the creamer to her chest, she closed the fridge and turned to find Harry standing right there. He was close enough to touch, close enough to stretch on tiptoe to kiss that handsome, awkward mouth that had loved her so thoroughly. But she did neither. The mixture of pain and longing stamped on his chiseled features tore at her heart. "You've taken a big first step toward healing. But there are bound to be relapses. Fight through them. Accept that sometimes you're going to fail, then move on. You don't think I get depressed sometimes? That I don't get angry? Look at me yelling at poor Mr. Finch. You have to give it time."

"Time is one thing I don't have. If I don't get my head on right before I return to the Corps in six weeks, they won't take me." He captured a strand of hair that had fallen over her cheek and rubbed it between his thumb and fingers before smoothing it behind her ear and backing away. "Maybe no one should." He grabbed his coat and headed to the front door. "Lock yourself in with the dogs. I need to clear my head."

Daisy hurried after him. "You can't go for a walk with your foot cut up like that."

"Then I'll drive." He opened the front door and pointed to the lock behind him. "I'll be back by lunch. Anything happens, you call me or the cops."

"What if something happens to *you*?" That stopped him.

Then he tunneled his fingers into the hair at her nape, cupped the back of her neck and pulled her onto her toes for a hard, potent kiss. He kissed her a second time. And a third. "I'll think about that. And how much I want…to be fixed. For you."

Chapter Ten

Harry returned two and a half hours later with several new strings of outdoor Christmas lights and an eight-foot Scotch pine tree for Daisy's living room. He'd also purchased a properly sized winter coat for himself in basic beige and a lavender parka with a bow on the belt he guessed would be about Daisy's size. The thank you hugs were a nice bonus, but he hadn't let her smile or welcoming arms sway him from his mission. He had something to prove, not only to Daisy, but to himself.

This time, he hadn't hiked through the snow or spent a couple of hours breathing fresh air. Sure, he'd driven around the neighborhood for about ten minutes, thinking he needed to clear his head. But then he realized he didn't need to clear anything— he needed to accept everything that was jumbled up inside him and attack it with a plan. He needed to think like a marine.

Protect the base. Get intel. Know your enemy. Trust your allies.

He'd called Pike to drive over and keep an eye on

Daisy's house while he was gone. Then he'd asked his brother-in-law about the photos he'd taken, and ended up talking to one of his friends, a Detective Nick Fensom, who was familiar with Daisy's assault case. The detective confirmed to Harry's own peace of mind that Daisy's ex was still incarcerated, and that the people around her, Bernie and Stella Riley, Angelo and Albert Logan, didn't have criminal records. Nick reminded Harry that just because a person didn't have a record, it didn't mean he or she didn't have it in for Daisy. She might be the stalker's first target, or he simply hadn't been reported or caught for this kind of behavior previously.

Detective Fensom also wanted to know more about the threats she'd been receiving, and promised to contact both the Central Prep principal, Ryan Hague, and John Murdock at the KCFD to get details on the events that had happened at the school. Fensom also wanted to document the messages and gifts Daisy had received, along with a timeline so he could put together a case against her stalker once he was caught. And he would be caught, if Harry had anything to do with it.

When he got back to the house, Pike and his son, Gideon, were building a snowman in the front yard, away from where the shards of broken bulbs still littered the snow. Hope was in the kitchen helping Daisy fix them all some lunch. By the time Gideon and Hope lay down for afternoon naps, he and Pike had put up the Christmas tree, swept off the deck and put all the dogs through their paces in the backyard.

Caliban was an old pro, slow but responsive to each command. Patch picked up on the training quickly, even learning a couple of new tricks. And Muffy was, well, what the dog lacked in attention span he made up for in personality. The misnamed Shih Tzu was never going to make it in the K-9 Corps, but he sure knew how to sound an alarm. Whether he was letting them know that Albert and Angelo had arrived to help clean up the yard, or he was chasing a bird off the fence, Muffy had something to say about it.

After they ordered pizza and finished dinner, Hope and her family and the two teenagers left. Trying to remember that he was the tenant/bodyguard and not the crazy boyfriend who wanted to peel the bright red Chiefs sweatshirt and matching glasses off Daisy and see if the miracle of last night had been a fluke, he put the dogs out, checked the locks, then resolutely ignored Daisy's blue-eyed disappointment and went upstairs to shower and get whatever sleep he could.

After his shopping trip that morning, he'd also come back with personal supplies he needed to put away, and a wood train set for his nephew that he hid on the top shelf of his closet until he could get it wrapped. All in all, it was a productive day. A healthy, normal, "worn out by work instead of an ongoing mental battle" kind of day. He hadn't wigged out and he hadn't hurt anyone.

Now if he could do this again tomorrow. And the day after that.

Harry toweled off and pulled on a clean pair of shorts and the faded USMC sweatpants he slept in. The lights were off downstairs and Daisy and the dogs had gone to bed. Alone in the soothing quiet, he stowed his service Beretta in the nightstand and dumped out his recent purchases on the bed. He packed the fresh bar of soap, disposable razors and condoms in his toiletry bag, set the pack of gum on the dresser beside his wallet, and opened the box of bandages and antibiotic salve before sitting down to redress the cuts on his feet. None of them were bad enough to need stitches, but an infection was the last thing he needed right now. When he'd finished medic duty, he folded down the quilt, piled the pillows against the headboard and picked up the package of ink pens and the spiral notebook he'd bought.

This was going to be the hard part.

Harry flipped open the notebook and stared at the blank piece of paper. He breathed deeply, steeling himself for the task at hand. He might not be a natural talent for this relationship stuff, or understand the intricate workings of the human brain, but he knew how to follow orders.

He started writing.

Day one. Mission accomplished.

A list was easier than coming up with sentences and paragraphs. He stated his objectives, and how well he'd met them.

Lt. Col. Biro had ordered him to get a Christmas tree and eat too many sweets. Check and check.

The lieutenant colonel had also ordered him to

kiss a pretty girl. Definitely a check. Multiple checks. If he succeeded with this plan of action, he hoped to fill up this entire notebook with check marks on that assignment.

But for now, he'd sustain himself on the memory of Daisy's patience with him, her acceptance of his scars, her passionate abandon to touch and be touched that forced him to tip his head back and breathe deeply to cool his body's desire to march down those stairs to be with her again. She'd probably welcome him to her bed because she was Daisy—the woman who cared too much and forgave too easily. But Harry had every intention of proving he was worthy of that compassion and forgiveness before indulging his physical needs. He didn't want to be another rescue mission for her. He wanted to be a whole man—one who never left her second-guessing her willingness to trust him. He wanted to be a man she could love without any regrets.

The objective was clear. Follow orders. Complete the mission.

Back to the notebook.

Dr. Polk had advised him to get plenty of exercise, journal his thoughts and keep his appointments. Check. Check. Check.

Daisy said to write her letters.

Harry hesitated. What exactly was he supposed to say to her that wouldn't sound pitiful or controlling or downright scary?

He clipped the pen onto the paper and rolled out of bed to do twenty reps on the pull-up bar he'd hung over the door. When he focused on the burning muscles, the memories in his head sorted themselves.

Daisy liked to talk. And if he was a smart man, he would listen.

You're giving me value by trusting me with your fears, by sharing your darkest feelings, by helping me understand you.

He went back to the bed, turned to a new page in the notebook and started writing.

Dear Daisy...

HARRY LED A normal life for the next four days.

He drove Daisy to school and picked her up afterward. He restocked her groceries and took out her trash. He spent a long two hours babysitting Gideon so that Hope could take a break and have lunch with a friend. He and Daisy met with Nick Fensom in her classroom, handing over the evidence from her desk and briefing the detective on anyone she suspected.

Since his feet were too sore to do a daily run, Harry put the dogs in the truck and hauled them to a dog park for a good workout. He discovered Patch had an affinity for catching flying discs and Albert Logan had an interest in learning more about training dogs. He'd picked up Albert after a tutoring session with Daisy and brought him to the house to teach the young man some of the skills he'd learned as a handler. He took Daisy out to dinner one night on a real date, even kissing her good-night at the front door before heading upstairs to his room as if they were getting newly acquainted. Daisy was frustrated with the distance he was keeping. The frustrated desire was wearing on him, too. "I'm trying to get your Harry back," he promised her. Ultimately, she seemed to understand that he needed to do this and gave him the space he asked for.

There were no more messages from Secret Santa, no odious gifts delivered. Bernie Riley kept his promise and stopped leaving items for her at school. The quiet spell seemed to back up Riley's claim that someone had been swapping out the innocent gifts his wife had picked out with the cruel taunts and graphic images. Daisy wanted to believe that, with no outlet, the threats had stopped for good. But neither she nor Harry really did. This was simply the calm before the storm. Harry suspected that, like an enemy whose line of propaganda had been cut off, the pervert's frustration was building like a volcano about to erupt. Without a daily avenue to get his message across to Daisy, he was probably planning something even bigger and more terrifying to grab her attention. Harry intended to be ready to protect her from whatever that threat might be.

Harry might be broken inside, but he'd been trained to adapt and overcome to get the job done. If his job was proving to Daisy, and more importantly to himself, that he was healthy relationship material, then he was going to do whatever it took to make that happen.

Including writing in that spiral notebook every night.

Some of the entries were horrible, angry scratches

that cut through five sheets of paper. Some were just a report of his day—his successes and his failures. The fresh batches of cookies he'd volunteered to sample. The training sessions with the dogs. Working with Angelo and Albert to move some furniture and crates into the garage and finish a couple of painting projects before the Christmas party, when the house would be invaded by thirty-seven teachers and staff, along with their significant others.

His chest got tight just thinking about a crowd of noisy revelers invading Daisy's home. If Secret Santa was one of her coworkers, would he try something that night? Or would he wait until he had a private time and place to finish whatever he had in mind for Daisy?

Tonight, those troubling thoughts about where all this was headed had morphed into a nightmare. Sitting bolt upright in a cold sweat, Harry kicked back the covers that had twisted around his legs and cursed the darkness. He flipped on the lamp beside him and focused on it, inhaling several cooling breaths. He didn't know how long he'd been thrashing in the bed, or if he'd been swearing out loud in his sleep, but he'd been caught up in a dream long enough to have knocked a pillow, his cell phone and the notebook to the floor. He straightened the mess and picked up his pen.

14 December 3:17 a.m.
Dear Daisy,
Thought I was having a good day today. But

you were right. Relapses happen and suddenly I'm in the middle of a nightmare. I know it's just in my head. But the fear felt pretty damn real.

You were in that fire again. Only, I couldn't get to you. I don't know what's wrong with my brain that it can only picture the worst. Why aren't I dreaming about the way your blue eyes squint me into focus when you want something from me? Or the way they darkened like midnight when you flew apart all around me? Any other guy would be dreaming about the sex. And don't think I haven't imagined being with you again.

But no, my brain took you with me when I went back to that firefight with the IEDs going off. I had Tango in my arms that day, and I guess a lot of the blood I saw on him was my own. But it all got jumbled up and I was holding you and there was nothing but blood and fire. I couldn't see your smile. I couldn't hear your laugh. I couldn't stop screaming.

The smell of burning skin is an awful, awful...

A soft metallic clinking noise turned Harry's attention to the door. Any mild sense of alarm that he hadn't detected the noise sooner ebbed when he identified the familiar sound of jangling dog tags and the click, click, click of paws slowly coming up the stairs. Who was making the rounds tonight? "Patch? Fur ball?"

He slept with the door open so that he'd be able to hear anything happening on the ground floor he needed to investigate. But he was unprepared for the furry gray muzzle peeking around the door frame or the Belgian Malinois panting for breath as he stared at Harry from the doorway.

"Caliban?" The dog's dark ears pricked up with recognition. For a brief moment, Tango's dark muzzle superimposed itself over the old dog's face. Harry blinked and Caliban returned. But the same heart and spirit remained in those dark brown eyes. "You worried about me, buddy?" The dog cocked his head to one side as if they were having a conversation and Harry chuckled. "I would be, too." He tossed the notebook aside. "Come here, boy. *Hier.*" Caliban trotted over in his rolling gait and Harry patted the top of the mattress, inviting him up beside him. *"Hopp."*

When Caliban jumped up onto the quilt, Harry rewarded him with a little bit of wrestling that ended with a tummy rub and him smiling. "Good boy. I guess those sharp old ears heard me." Caliban thrust his front paw into the air so that Harry could scratch the leg pit there. "You're used to looking out for a partner. And now you're looking out for me."

The nightmare faded and some good memories of his time with Tango made his eyes gritty with tears. "Tango used to wake me up when I got to tossing and turning too much, too. You lost your partner and I lost mine. We'll look out for each other, okay?"

Caliban rolled onto his belly, sitting up like a Sphinx and eyeing the door.

Harry swung his legs off the edge of the bed. "I hear it, too."

A parade of dog paws rushing up the stairs, followed by the noise of creaking wood as someone slightly heavier hurried behind them. Muffy and Patch dashed in and jumped right up on the bed, jockeying for petting position beside him. "Hello, you two."

At the last second, he remembered to shove his notebook out of sight under his pillow before rising to meet Daisy when she appeared in the doorway.

"Hello." Her hair was tousled and sexy, she had a wrinkle on her cheek from her pillow, and she was wearing those shapeless flannel pajamas that were almost as soft as her skin. The hungry sweep of her gaze over his bare chest intensified the gut-kick of desire already rushing through his blood and threatened to undo every well-planned good intention of his recovery mission. He pushed the excited dogs away and took a step closer. "Did I wake you?" Dumb question. Clearly, she was worried about him.

"You mean the headboard banging against the wall up here?" She held up her thumb and forefinger pinched together. "Little bit."

"Sorry." He nodded over his shoulder. "Caliban came up to…"

"Are you all right?"

Her question topped his statement and they both fell silent.

Daisy hugged her arms beneath her breasts and nodded toward the three-legged dog. "When I woke up, I realized he was missing. This is the last place I would have looked if I hadn't heard you. He's never come up the stairs before. He must really like you."

"He probably recognizes a kindred spirit."

She wasn't wearing her robe or those fuzzy slipper socks. As she drew invisible circles on the hardwood with her big toe, he noticed something he hadn't before. She painted her toenails. Purple, like the highlights in her hair. It was hard to remember the way he'd first pictured Daisy—the golden angel dressed in white and bathed in sunshine. The real Daisy was meant for moonlight and bold color and ill-timed fantasies in the middle of the night.

"Do you need to talk about it? The nightmare?"

"I'm not dumping on you."

The circles stopped. "It's not dumping. It's one friend listening to another."

"No."

"What about your therapist? Or your sister?" Her shoulders puffed up with a sigh and she kept talking. "I know you're on some kind of healing journey. You're afraid that you're going to scare me or hurt me or make me worry too much. Well, I'm always going to worry about you. That's what people who care about each other do, so you're not doing me any favors by isolating yourself."

"I am not dumping on you." When her blue eyes

peeked above the rims of her glasses, he put up his hands and tried to reassure her. "But I'm not bottling it all up inside, either. I'm following doctor's orders. And Lieutenant Colonel Biro's orders. And… your orders."

"Mine?"

"Something you said the other night. I've been writing letters."

"To me?"

"In a journal of sorts." Muffy knocked aside his pillow to claim a spot on the bed, and revealed his secret. "Thanks for ratting me out, fur ball." Harry picked up the pillow and set the spiral notebook on the bedside table. "I don't know if anyone is ever going to read it. But it helps to get it out."

"I'm proud of you, Harry. I know it can't be easy."

"It's important to me that I'm in control of myself— how I react to people, how I treat you—before I let you and me go any further." He'd already given her his heart—there wasn't much further he could go. But he didn't want to ruin the best thing that had ever happened to him before it had even gotten started. "The dream tonight kind of rattled me. Made me think that I wasn't the right man to protect you."

"Harry, I don't want—"

He pressed a finger against her lips to silence her argument. "I make no claims to be a hundred percent yet. But I'm not trusting anyone else with the job of keeping you safe."

"Okay," she murmured beneath his finger. "May I talk now?"

He lingered a little longer where he shouldn't before curling his fingers into his palm and pulling away. "I needed you to understand that."

"There's no one I trust more to protect me. I just wish you'd let me do something for you in return."

Maybe there was something. "Could I hold you for a while? After what I saw, I won't be able to sleep unless I know you're safe. And the only way I can know that when I'm dozing off is to—"

She walked straight into his chest and wrapped her arms around his waist. Her forehead found that familiar spot against his neck and she softened against him, fitting all her curves to his harder planes. "I can stay."

Feeling the tension of his nightmare leaving his body already, Harry wound his arms around her to complete the hug and nestled his nose against her hair. "Just to sleep, honey." He was reminding his own body's eager response to her touch, as much as clarifying the request for her. "You've got school tomorrow morning."

"I am happy to hold and be held by you anytime, Harry Lockhart." She pressed her lips to the scar beneath his collarbone. "Do you think I've been getting good sleep downstairs by myself? I need you close by so I know you're safe, too."

They stood like that until Harry's body began to respond in a way he hadn't intended. Forcing himself to pull away, he led her to the bed and tucked her under the covers. After setting her glasses aside, he claimed the spot Muffy wanted, lay down on top of the quilt and pulled Daisy into his arms. As the three dogs settled in behind her and at the foot of the bed, Harry reached over and turned off the lamp.

"This is better," she whispered, resting her head on his shoulder.

"Much better."

Daisy and the dogs were all asleep when Harry heard a car door slamming outside. He gently extricated himself from the arm around his waist and went to the front and side windows to peek through the curtains. He scanned up and down the block, looking for the exhaust from a running car or any signs of movement. But there was nothing suspicious—no one in her yard or walking the street. He went across the hall and looked out the bathroom window to see if the new motion detector light he'd installed over the deck had come on. But the back of the house was dark and still. No heartbroken teenager busting up the new lights, no one throwing snowballs at the house or standing outside her bedroom window.

By the time Harry returned, Caliban had raised his head in curiosity, but wasn't alerting to any signs of an intruder. Muffy would certainly be going off if someone was trying to break in. Harry petted the Malinois and climbed back into bed. The house was locked up tight. His gun was in arm's reach and Daisy was tucked safely in his arms.

If the dogs weren't worried about one lone sound in the night, he wouldn't be, either.

EVEN IF DAISY was willing to risk a little PDA in front of the students hurrying through the front doors for a morning practice or the breakfast program, the dogs wedged between her and Harry in the front seat of his truck would have prevented it.

"You're spoiling them," she teased, pulling Muffy back to her lap to avoid the Shih Tzu's marauding tongue. She was pleased to see that Caliban had claimed his spot beside Harry on the bench seat. The older dog had perked up in both energy and personality since Harry had moved into the house. Patch stood with his front paws on the dashboard, wagging his little bob of a tail and watching the students and staff walk past the truck in the circular driveway. He just wanted to be a part of what everyone else was doing. "You've been to the dog park every morning this week."

Harry rubbed his hand around Caliban's ears. "It gives me a little exercise, too. Plus, there aren't a lot of people there this time of year."

"Do you think you'll ever be able to tolerate crowds again?"

"Who knows? I'm a work in progress." He shifted his petting hand to Patch, who instantly crawled over Caliban to sit in Harry's lap. His stiff half smile faded as he turned his attention to the people walking past. "Look at all the blue coats and yellow caps going into Central Prep. Maybe you should invite me to speak to your classes."

"About what?"

"PTSD? My career in the military? How letter

writing is a lost art and they should be glad you're teaching it to them?"

She understood what Harry's sudden willingness to spend the day with a bunch of hormonal teenagers was really about. "So you can keep an eye on me?"

"Too controlling?"

She reached across the seat to pull his gloved hand off Patch and squeeze it. "You aren't Brock Jantzen."

He squeezed back. "I'm just trying to be a better Harry Lockhart."

"You know I'll be waiting for you whenever you're ready, right?"

"What if I'm never ready?"

Daisy wondered if never being Harry's woman would be worse than being the woman he had loved and left behind because he decided he couldn't do relationships, after all. But that was too heart-breaking a topic to discuss on this sunny winter morning when Harry was fighting like everything to find his new normal. She smiled, instead, pulling her hand away to adjust Muffy's red sweater. "Fridays I don't have to stay late, so be here at three-thirty."

"Yes, ma'am. On the dot."

Daisy dumped Muffy off her lap and looped her pink bag over her shoulder. "Have a good day, Top."

"Be safe, Ms. G." When she turned to assure him she would, he was already leaning in. "Come here," he growled.

His firm lips scudded across hers in a searing kiss. His touch warmed her all the way down to the toes of her boots. Not that she'd ever complained, but he was growing more confident, less self-conscious with every kiss. Daisy touched her fingers to his jaw and would have encouraged him to explore his craft to his heart's content, but there were suddenly cold noses and warm tongues trying to join in.

"Blecch." Daisy flattened her hand between them to ward off the licks on her neck and chin while Harry retreated to his side of the truck, his deep chest bouncing with laughter. Daisy joined him. A genuine laugh from Harry was worth a hundred kisses.

She opened the truck door and climbed out. "Bye."

Daisy walked through a gauntlet of "woo-hoos" and whistles, and a couple of thumbs-ups from students and staff as she headed inside and crossed through the lobby. "You people need to go study," she admonished, hoping they'd mistake the blush on her cheeks as a sign of the cold morning air and not her happy embarrassment.

She ran into Mary Gamblin in the teachers' lounge and poured herself a mug of coffee before walking down the hallway to their rooms together. "Are you still feeling up to that party tomorrow?" Mary asked. "With everything that's going on, isn't it stressing you out?"

"No," Daisy answered honestly. "It gives me something fun and positive to focus on. You better come and help me eat all the cookies I've baked this week. If everybody doesn't bring the potluck dishes they signed up for, we're all going to be on a massive sugar high by the end of the evening."

"It's good to see you in a happy mood again. Does

it have anything to do with that marine you were kissing out front?"

There was no masking the blush on her cheeks this time. "Did everybody see that?"

"Enough people to start the rumor mill."

Daisy nudged her shoulder against her friend's, refusing to be the only fodder for gossip today. "What about you? Are you and Eddie coming to the party together?"

"I had to drop about every hint I could." Mary rolled her eyes and giggled. "But yeah. He asked me."

"Awesome." They reached their respective rooms across the hall from each other and inserted their keys into the locks. "Hey, I hung some mistletoe if you'd like to take advantage…"

"He's a slow mover."

"Maybe a Christmas kiss will help him move a little faster."

"Fingers crossed." They pushed open their doors. "Have a good day."

"You, too."

Once inside her room, Daisy turned on the lights and unhooked the lavender bow on her coat, unbuttoning the gift from Harry as she crossed to the front of the room to her desk. She set her coffee on the corner and pulled out her chair.

And froze.

No. Whatever she was feeling right now went beyond freezing. She couldn't think. Couldn't move. Couldn't feel.

Her bag dropped to the floor beside her. She stared at the neatly-wrapped oblong box lying on the seat of her chair. Decorated with an all too familiar card emblazoned with a sparkly green tree, the present taunted her with its ominous promise.

As the feeling returned to her limbs, she leaned over to read the words typed across the face of the card.

Get rid of him! Or I will.
You belong to me.
Merry Christmas from your Secret Santa.

"Oh, my God." A righteous anger suddenly flowed through her body, giving her the strength to move. Leaving her gloves on in case her tormentor had slipped up this time and left fingerprints, she picked up the box, finding it surprisingly heavy for its size. She dropped it onto the middle of her blotter and stooped down to dig her phone out of her purse.

Her first instinct was to call Harry. She needed him here with her. Now. Nobody else understood, nobody else cared as much, about how terrified she was of her stalker. She needed his arms. His growly comforts and complaints. His do-the-job-or-die attitude to make the terror go away.

Her hands were shaking as she pulled up the call screen. But it was pointless to pull up her list of contacts as she remembered they were more about touching and talking in person, and had been together so much of the past week that she hadn't needed to call him. Until she needed to call him. Like now. Daisy pushed to her feet. "Even if you can never say you love me, you are going to give me your phone number, damn it."

But the flare of anger, aimed mostly at herself, quickly abated. Red liquid was seeping through the wrapping paper from a corner of the box she must have bent when she'd dropped it. The liquid, viscous and thick, spread across the white blotter, creating a crimson puddle in the middle of her desk.

"Please don't be..." She untied the bow and lifted the lid. She squeezed her hand over her mouth, fighting back the urge to scream. The box held a soldier action figure, his face blacked out with ink. The whole thing was sitting in a pool of red liquid that could only be one thing. Blood.

Animal blood. Fake blood. A grotesque pint from her stalker, it didn't matter. Daisy turned away from the gruesome gift and swiped her hand across her phone, dialing 9-1-1. She needed to notify Mr. Hague, too. And more than anything, she needed to get a hold of Harry.

"9-1-1. What is the nature of your emergency?"

"My name is Daisy Gunderson. I'm a teacher at Central Prep Academy."

The bell rang and the hallway filled with noise as students came up the stairs and went to their lockers.

Daisy plugged her finger over her free ear and raised her voice. "Can you connect me directly to Detective Nick Fensom? Or take a report that will get to him? He's investigating a case for me and there's been another incident."

"It looks like Detective Fensom is attached to the Fourth Precinct. If this isn't an emergency, let me…."

Locker doors slammed and chatting students filtered into the classroom. "I'm sorry. Could you repeat that?"

"Yo, Ms. G."

"Do we have to take that test today?"

"How much of it is essay?"

She turned away from the friendly greetings and typical questions as the students came in, some automatically stuffing their phones into the shoe bag by the door, others gawking at the crude gift sitting in a puddle of blood on her desk.

"Ms. G., you can't have your cell phone in class."

"What is that?"

"Gross!"

She shushed the teasing and cringing so she could make her report.

And that's when the intercom over the door crackled to life and Mr. Hague made an announcement. "Attention, staff. Mr. Brown is in the building. I repeat, Mr. Brown is in the building. This is not a drill."

The students looked at each other. Some of the young faces were grave, others panicked a bit. A few were blessedly oblivious to the significance of the announcement.

"Everybody line up," Daisy ordered, pulling her phone from her ear. She picked up her attendance sheet, counted heads and quickly took roll. "Twenty. Twenty-one." All but one student accounted for. "Have any of you seen Angelo?"

There was a flurry of "nos" and "I-thought-I-saws" that were no help at all. "Somebody text him or call."

She opened her desk drawer to pull out her walkie-talkie for school emergencies, but it, too, was missing.

"He's not answering, Ms. G."

"He may not have his phone turned on. He knows you're not supposed to at school."

"Shouldn't we be going? Ms. Gamblin's class is leaving."

Daisy nodded. "If we pass your locker on the way out the door, you can grab your coat. Otherwise, keep moving." She searched two more drawers, knowing this was no drill, knowing they were all in serious trouble.

"Are you coming, Ms. G.?"

"I'm right behind you." She waved her class out the door. "Go."

She rummaged through the last two drawers. Secret Santa hadn't just left her the gift. He'd taken her walkie-talkie, isolating her from instant contact with the rest of the staff.

As per every evacuation, the fire alarm went off in a loud, continuous ringing, and Daisy's blood ran cold with fear. This was it. She felt it in her bones. Her fate was sealed.

"Ma'am, are you still there?" The dispatcher was prompting her to respond. She grabbed the clipboard with everyone's name and put the phone back to her ear. "My screen shows that we've already received a call from a Ryan Hague at that same location. Is this in relation to that call?"

Daisy mentally checked off the names on her list as each student filed past. But there was still one missing. It was too early in the day to have received the absentee list. She had to account for Angelo's location. "Down the stairs and out the door. Don't stop until you get to the church across the street."

"Ma'am? Are you there?"

Mr. Brown meant only one thing.

"Yes. There may be a bomb in the building."

Chapter Eleven

"Gunderson."

Daisy stopped her march toward the stairs and turned toward the summons. "Coach? What are you doing up here on the second floor?"

"Health class. Borrowing Musil's room since it's her free period. Showing a video—the kind you want a little more privacy for than in the gym." She scooted a group of students on past her and waited for Bernie to catch up before continuing toward the exit beside him. "Kind of sucky that I picked today of all days to borrow a room that's on the top floor." He snapped his fingers and pointed a young woman away from her locker. "Keep moving."

The frightened young woman linked arms with a friend and hurried to catch up with their classmates. "Slow down," Daisy reminded them, ducking away from the flashing light and deafening noise of the alarm as they walked past. "We want everyone to get there in one piece."

"Are we really taking all these kids outside in this weather?" Bernie asked.

"It's not a drill." Daisy lowered her voice so the students wouldn't overhear. "I just got off the phone with the 9-1-1 operator. Mr. Hague called them about a bomb threat."

Bernie let out a low whistle. "Somebody wanted Christmas vacation early, huh?"

More likely *somebody* didn't think she was frightened enough by threatening just her. Harry had been right about the violence escalating. Now her Secret Santa was threatening the people around her—the people she cared about—her students, friends and coworkers, Harry himself. And she had accused Harry of trying to control her. What an idiot. At least he had a legitimate reason for the pronouncements and territorial behavior—he was trying to protect her. Even Brock's obsession had never extended to hurting anyone beyond her.

Secret Santa had taken her life to a whole new level of scary this morning.

"My walkie-talkie is missing," she told Bernie. It was far easier to focus on her responsibilities as a teacher than to let one man's obsession get into her head and paralyze her with fear. "Will you call the office and find out if Angelo is absent today?"

"Don't have to. He's here."

"He wasn't in my first period class."

Bernie stopped in his tracks, muttering a curse that left a couple of students near the back of the line tittering at the grownup breaking a school rule. "They're cutting class now? That's the last thing Albert needs to do."

"But you saw them," Daisy clarified.

"Yeah. I had both brothers in my office before school to talk about putting Albert back on the team after the holidays. Part of Angelo's penance for the vandalism at your place will be helping his brother keep his grades up."

"Where is Albert now? Could they still be together? Maybe they've already exited the building with another group."

"I can find out."

"Mary? Ms. Gamblin?" Daisy dashed ahead to catch her friend at the top of the stairs and hand over her student roster. "Will you take my class with yours to the church? We have two missing students. The Logan twins."

"Of course." Mary herded both classes down the steps ahead of her. "Need any help?"

"We've got it covered. Just keep my kids safe." Daisy hurried back to Bernie, who was putting out an all call on the walkie-talkie on the missing student. "Who's got Albert Logan first hour?"

"I do," the answer crackled over the radio.

Recognizing the voice, Daisy pulled Bernie's device down to her level. "Eddie? Was Albert in class? Did you see Angelo with him?"

"No and no." Eddie Bosch sounded slightly breathless. "My chemistry class is already across the street. I'm running back in to look for him. I'll have to do a room-by-room search, including bathrooms and closets."

What were those boys up to? "I'm responsible for Angelo. I can help. What floor are you on?"

"I'll start in the basement and work my way up."

"I'll start on the second floor. I've got Bernie Riley with me."

The tall man nodded and put the radio back up to his mouth. "I'll check the first floor. Riley out."

"Bosch out."

Bernie caught Daisy by the shoulder and squeezed. "Will you be okay up here? You don't have a walkie-talkie."

She held up her phone. "I've got 9-1-1. As soon as you've cleared your floor, get out of here. I plan to do the same."

"All right." Bernie squeezed her arm again before releasing her. "Hague will be on the first floor, waiting for the first responders. I'll tell him that you, Bosch and I are still inside looking for the Logans. Meet me in the faculty parking lot when you're done so I know you're out of the building. Be careful."

"You, too."

He jogged down the stairs after the last of the students and disappeared around the corner of the landing.

Other than the jarring noise of the fire alarm, everything was a lot quieter now that the second floor had been evacuated and the main floor was emptying out. "Angelo? Albert?" Just like in their summer emergency training workshop, Daisy moved methodically down one side of the hallway, opening every door. "It's Ms. G. This isn't a drill. We need to evacuate the building."

When she reached the end of one row of classrooms, she crossed the hall and repeated the same search. "Is anyone up here?"

She reentered her own classroom, avoiding even an accidental glance at the bloody mess on her desk, and walked straight to her closet. Empty. There were only two classrooms left to search up here. There was probably a perfectly reasonable explanation for the missing twins. Maybe they'd never reached their first period classes and had been ushered outside by the first teacher who'd spotted them. But that teacher should have reported that they had them by now. Of course, without a radio, she wouldn't know if they'd been found. Best to keep moving, clear her floor and get outside.

She kept her focus out the bank of windows as she headed back toward the front of the room. From this vantage point, she could see the white steeple rising above the red brick church, and a sea of blue and gold Central Prep colors flowing slowly but steadily through the church's front doors. Maybe she'd be able to find the Logans once she was at the church with the rest of the evacuees, and they'd separated into their classes again in the various Sunday School rooms.

A latent image sharpened into focus and Daisy rushed back to the windows, wiping the condensation from the glass and peering closer. She recognized a loose-limbed stride and dark brown head. "Angelo?

Albert?" She knocked against the window, knowing the church was too far away for anyone there to hear her. She could barely hear herself over the incessant ring of the fire alarm. Which one of the boys was that? With similar faces and matching uniforms, it was impossible to tell at this distance.

But she was certain she'd just spotted one of them. She pulled her cell phone from the pocket of her coat. Who should she call? She didn't keep student numbers in her phone. 9-1-1 would take too long. She needed an instant response. She could call one of the other teachers to track down the Logan she'd seen. But which one?

Daisy finally punched in her boss's number and hurried out the door. As the man coordinating the evacuation with KCFD and the police, he would definitely have his cell on him. When the principal answered, she quickly updated him. "I'm the last person on the second floor and I'm on my way down to the rear parking lot exit. I swear I just saw one of the Logan boys crossing the street to the church. Could you get someone down there to verify that for me?"

"Why aren't you on your radio?" Mr. Hague asked.

"*He* took it. I'm certain of it."

"He? The man sending you those messages?"

She entered the last room and checked the closet. "There was another gift on my desk this morning. Maybe the sickest one yet. I'm sorry, sir. I think this bomb threat is all about me. I never thought he'd endanger anyone else."

"I'll notify the police about your suspicions. Just get out of the building. I'll call as soon as I hear anything about the Logan boys."

"Thank you, sir."

After disconnecting the call, Daisy hurried down the steps and walked as quickly as she dared without breaking into a run like the girls she'd chastised earlier.

But someone *was* running through the hallway.

"Daisy? Thank God, I caught you." She stopped and turned as Eddie Bosch jogged up to her. He grabbed her by both shoulders and gently shook her. "Why aren't you answering your radio? I thought something had happened to you."

Reaching up, she gave his wrist a squeeze of gratitude for his concern. "That sick Secret Santa of mine took it. He left me another present this morning."

"How bad?"

"Bad enough." She turned toward the exit, expecting him to walk with her. "Let's talk outside. I want to get to the church. I spotted one of the Logan boys there. Get on your radio and ask which Logan it is."

"It's Angelo."

She stopped again, frowning to see that he hadn't followed her. "How do you know?"

"Because I found Albert."

"That's wonderful news. Did you send him across the street?" When Eddie didn't immediately answer, she closed the distance between them. "What's wrong?"

"Albert is in the basement. He won't leave until

he talks to you. Something about apologizing and doing right by you."

"That's ridiculous. Tell him to get his butt up here. I'll talk to him about anything—" she thumbed over her shoulder "—at the church."

"You don't understand."

"No, I don't." Why wasn't he moving?

"The bomb is real. I saw it with my own eyes."

Daisy shrank back at his grim declaration, hugging herself as an invisible chill washed over her. She'd known in her heart that this was no drill. But a real bomb? "I'd hoped it was just a threat."

Eddie shook his head. "I reported the location to Mr. Hague."

"Then we need to get Albert and go." She darted past him, moving toward the basement stairs.

But Eddie grabbed her arm and stopped her. "Maybe we should just let the police handle it."

Bernie Riley's voice cut through the static on Eddie's radio. "First floor is clear. If anyone has eyes on Ms. G., tell her I'm on my way out to meet her."

Eddie held up his radio. "Why are you meeting him?"

Daisy tugged her arm free. "He knows I don't have a walkie-talkie. We made a plan so that someone could confirm I was out of the building and the evacuation was complete."

"A plan? When did you talk to him? Where did you see him? His office and the gym are on the opposite side of the building from your classroom."

Daisy was backing away, needing to make sure

one last student was safe. "A few minutes ago. Up-stairs."

"You don't think that's suspicious? When did Coach Riley ever do something that benefitted any-body but himself?"

Bernie's explanation had been plausible. He'd had his class upstairs with him. But she supposed that could have been a cover. It would have certainly put him a lot closer to her room to leave that gift and steal her radio without being seen.

"You think Bernie is..." Daisy clenched her fists, shaking off the distracting thoughts. "Eddie, please. Either leave or come help me convince Albert to evacuate. This is my fault. That creeper who's after me—he's responsible. He can threaten me all he wants, but I am not going to let him hurt one of my students."

"Daisy." Eddie grabbed her by the wrist again, and she groaned with frustration. "The reason I couldn't get Albert to come with me..."

"What?"

"He's the one with the bomb."

HARRY PULLED OVER and slowed his truck as a third fire engine sped past in the oncoming lane. He didn't need Muffy sitting in his lap, barking at every flash-ing light, for the hackles on the back of his neck to go up.

Emergency vehicles didn't necessarily mean Daisy was in danger. There were other businesses and residential neighborhoods in that direction.

There could have been an unfortunate vehicle accident.

Muffy spotted another speeding car and threw his paws against the window to bark at it. The fire chief this time. There were more sirens and flashing lights farther down the road, speeding toward them as if that part of Kansas City was under attack.

Speeding toward Central Prep Academy.

Toward Daisy.

Toward the woman he loved.

"Anybody else got a bad feeling about this?"

Muffy gave a sharp yelp as if the little dingbat understood the urgency firing through his blood. The rest of the troops were in agreement.

He could be wrong. The fractured bits of his brains had messed with his perception of the truth lately. But neither a dog, nor his gut, had ever once given him bad intel. And if Daisy was in trouble, he couldn't run away from the fight.

Harry made a U-turn at the next intersection, pulled his Beretta from the glove compartment, and raced back to the school.

DAISY KNEW IT was a trap the moment her foot touched the basement's concrete floor. The stairs had been cordoned off with yellow crime scene tape from the fire, but someone had torn through it and come down the steps.

"Hold up," Eddie warned her from the top of the stairs. He'd been trying to raise Bernie on his radio to tell him that she and Eddie were tracking down Albert. "Coach isn't answering. Daisy?"

"Tell whoever's listening that we need an ambulance."

The door to the storage room had been propped open with a concrete bucket, and the entire locking mechanism had been removed. The char marks had been painted over with more of that gloomy gray paint. But a fresh coat of paint couldn't hide the reminder of one man's obsession with her.

Mine.

She was frozen in place—her blood, her breathing, the sharpness of her senses locking up with fear. And while she desperately wanted to turn right around and run up those stairs and out the front door, she couldn't. She couldn't run away from the trap, because she was a teacher, a caring person, a human being—and one of her students was lying unconscious in the middle of the floor. A gash dented his curly dark hair, and his yellow ball cap lay on the floor, soaking up the blood dripping from his head wound.

"Albert?" She forced her feet to move forward, slowly approaching his unmoving body, scanning all around him for any sign of the bomb or Bernie Riley. Albert hadn't made that bomb. He was as much of a pawn in all this madness as she was. And no one wielded more control over this young man than the coach. She was vaguely aware of Eddie relaying the request for medical help. If Eddie had seen Albert with the bomb, it hadn't been by choice. No doubt the young man had been coerced into giving Eddie, and subsequently her, a message that would not only keep her in the building, but bring her down here. "It's Ms. G. I'm here."

Seeing nothing that looked like a pipe or brief-case, like the bombs she'd seen on television shows and movies, she knelt beside him. She pulled back the collar of his team jacket and pressed her fingers against his neck. Thank God. He had a strong pulse. But he certainly wasn't able to answer any questions for her.

"Albert?" She petted the back of the unconscious teen's head. "I'm so sorry you got hurt. I'm going to get you out of here, okay?"

The sirens of the vehicles she heard pulling up outside reminded her that she wasn't alone. The noises also reminded her that it was far too quiet down here.

"Eddie? I need your help to move…" There was no answer. No sound of footsteps following her down the stairs. Had her friend abandoned her? Oh, God. Had something happened to him, too? "Mr. Bosch, answer me!"

Silence.

Daisy got up. But when she turned toward the storage room, she instantly retreated. Now *that* looked like something she'd seen in a movie.

There it was, sitting in the middle of the floor beside one of the folding metal chairs. A bomb. It was wire-y and liquid-y in clear tubes bound together with duct tape attached to a doughy-looking brick and a cell phone. The screen was flashing a series of numbers—32:26, 32:25, 32:24. A countdown. She didn't need to know how the thing worked. She just believed that it would.

"Oh, my God." She needed to call Harry. She needed him here. To hold her. To take charge. To make the fear go away.

She imagined the words in his letters, offering solutions. Assuring her that her problems could be fixed. Telling her that she had the power to do anything.

32:13

The bad guys don't get to win.

"We have to get out of here." Daisy hurried back to the fallen student.

She knew that moving an injured person wasn't the recommended procedure, but with a bomb ticking down just a few feet away, she'd make an exception. She wrapped her hands around Albert's wrists and pulled. His head lolled between his arms and he groaned as she dragged him toward the stairs. Good grief, he was heavy. Not just tall, but solidly built. When the back of her boot hit the bottom step, she gently lowered him to the floor and rolled him onto his back.

"Come on, Albert, wake up." She slipped her hands beneath his arms. With a mighty push of her legs, she got his bottom onto the first step before she had to set him down and lean him against the wall. Unless he regained consciousness, there was no way she was going to get him up these stairs. "Eddie?"

she shouted up the stairwell. "I need your help. Can anybody hear me?"

Maybe she shouldn't keep yelling. If something had happened to Eddie, then she was alone in the building with a man who equated rape and violence and fear with some sick kind of love. And she was only giving away her position to him.

"Ms. G.?" Albert slurred her name out on a moan of pain. "You gotta…"

"Albert?" She knelt beside him, capturing his face between her hands, willing his groggy brown eyes to stay open. "Can you stand if I help you?" His eyes drifted shut. "Albert!"

His eyes opened for one fierce warning. "Get out."

Something hard and unyielding whacked her in the back of the head. Fireworks exploded behind her eyes as she collapsed over Albert's body and everything went dark.

Chapter Twelve

Harry recognized a command center when he saw one. He could also identify the men in charge by the way everyone else scurried to do their bidding. He parked his truck behind the last police car in the circular driveway in front of Central Prep Academy and crossed the median to reach a group of men that included Daisy's principal, a black-haired cop in a SWAT uniform, John Murdock from the KCFD, Detective Nick Fensom and his brother-in-law, Pike.

SWAT? That explained the number of first responders.

His heart squeezed in his chest. Scenes like this were only supposed to happen in a war zone. He needed eyes on Daisy. Now.

Probably because he wore a gun like all the other cops here, and moved with an air of purpose and authority, no one stopped him until he reached the back of the SWAT van where the men in charge were going over building schematics and access points.

"Let him through." Nick Fensom waved him over. "He knows one of our hostages."

"Hostages?" He didn't bother asking if Daisy was safe. He knew she'd be in the thick of whatever was happening inside that building.

"We're not saying victims yet." John Murdock from the fire department exchanged a nod of recognition with Harry. "But our guy won't talk to us. He's cut off all communication. We don't have many details other than most of the students and staff have been evacuated and are safe in the church on the other side of the school."

"All he wants is Daisy." Of that, Harry was certain. "If anyone else has been hurt, it's collateral damage."

"Agreed." Nick scrubbed his hand over the dark stubble on his jaw. "Our concern is that when a stalker reaches this level of violence, he's usually got an end game."

He'd seen friends brought down by sniper bullets and roadside bombs. He'd lost part of his face and half his soul over in Iraq. Whatever Nick was trying to find a delicate way to say wouldn't shock him. "Meaning?"

"Most of these situations end in a murder/suicide."

"Like a suicide bomber. Or an insurgent waiting to detonate an IED when it'll do the most damage." Harry weathered the emotional punch of knowing Daisy was in a similarly volatile situation right now. He waited for the flashback to take hold, but it never came. This was a mission briefing. All he needed were his orders, and he could take action. Daisy was too important for him to sit on the sidelines and nurse his mental wounds or second-guess himself. He was getting better. He needed to be a part of this. "You said hostages, plural. This guy's got someone else in there with him?"

"One of the students," Pike answered. "We believe our perp used him as a decoy to bring Daisy to him."

"You got an ID on this guy?"

Pike shook his head. "There are two faculty members besides Daisy who haven't checked in yet—Bernard Riley and Edward Bosch. The student is Albert Logan."

"Unless Logan's our bomber?" Nick suggested.

"He's a good kid." Harry had worked with the teen enough this week to suspect Albert just needed the right thing to motivate him, and he'd turn his young life around. He'd had good instincts with the dogs, and had been interested enough to ask Harry where he'd gotten his training. "Rough around the edges. Makes some bad choices. But he wouldn't hurt Daisy. What about his brother?"

The principal piped in. "Angelo is fine. He and Albert were working with Coach Riley before school and were on their way to class when the bomb threat came in and I sounded the evacuation order. Angelo told one of the teachers at the church that Mr. Bosch asked Albert to help with a student who's wheelchair-bound. The handicapped student is accounted for. Angelo is pretty concerned that he hasn't seen his brother. I haven't told him about the hostage situation."

Harry had seen the pictures. He'd seen the fire. He'd seen the terror Daisy lived with every day because of that bastard. "You have to get her out of there. This guy's got a temper. He'll hurt her."

The nametag on the SWAT cop's uniform read *Delgado*. "We can't risk a full assault or he might blow everybody up."

Nick glanced around at all the swirling lights and imposing vehicles. "He already knows we're here. It's a little late for stealth mode."

"And, we don't know their exact location," John Murdock reminded them.

"They're in the basement," Harry said, knowing he was right on this. He was learning this enemy, and he wasn't all that unpredictable. "I don't know if the bomb is there, or if there's more than one. But that's where he'll be. With Daisy. I'm familiar with that area of the building, and one man won't be detected—especially if you're making some noise and talking at him out here. Let me go in." He turned to his brother-in-law. "You got some spare gear in your truck?"

"What are you thinking?"

"That I know how to find an insurgent and an IED."

In a matter of minutes, his credentials were approved and the plan was set. Harry went with Pike to his KCPD unit. They suited up in protective gear, while Pike's German shepherd, Hans, danced around inside his cage, sensing he was about to have a job to do. Donning the flak vest, gloves and helmet, Harry felt like he was slipping into a familiar uniform.

"Daisy means this much to you?" Pike asked.

"That woman saved me more than once. I owe it to her to do the same for her."

"You love her?"

Harry checked the radio unit on his vest and slipped a pair of protective goggles over his eyes, ignoring the question. He hadn't told Daisy how he felt yet, not in real words. Not out loud. It didn't feel right to say it to anybody else first.

Pike clapped him on the shoulder, forcing him to look at him. "You can't go in there if your head's not clear."

Harry pulled the extra K-9 ballistic vest from the back of Pike's truck. "Did you know you were in love with Hope before you rescued her from that jackass who kidnapped her?"

"Yes."

"Did it stop you from getting the job done?"

Pike grinned. "Hans and I will be ready to go in with SWAT as soon as you radio that you've secured the hostages. Just get them out. We'll clear the building, do a bomb sweep and neutralize the perp. Keep your com open so we know each other's twenty and don't have any surprises. You're okay to do this on your own?"

Harry went to his own pickup and opened the door, revealing Caliban in the passenger seat, eagerly sitting at attention. He slipped the vest over the dog's back and clipped it into place. "I won't be alone."

DAISY WOKE TO a hundred fireworks shooting off inside her head. Where was she? What had happened to her?

She mentally shook off the confusion and opened her eyes. She was surrounded by a sea of gray. And as she focused in on her outstretched arm, she saw spots of red on her new coat. Was that blood?

Wait. Blood?

The nightmare came flooding back. Albert. Bomb. *Mine.*

She pushed herself up to a sitting position. She was in the storage room, surrounded by windowless walls and stacked-up chairs.

"I've been waiting for you to come back to me."

Her groan was half headache, half heartache. She'd suspected a lot of people of stalking her over the last couple of weeks, but not this one. "Eddie?"

"Merry Christmas, my love."

He was sitting in a chair near her feet, holding two walkie-talkies in his lap, one which she suspected he'd stolen from her desk. He cradled a cell phone in his hands. Her cell phone. She raised her gaze above the blue school jacket and loosely knotted tie and saw a smear of pink lipstick across his mouth. Her color. She touched her fingers to her own mouth and cringed at the thought of him kissing her while she'd been unconscious—at the thought of him kissing her, period.

The bomb with the different colored liquids and ticking timer sat on the floor beside her. Instinctively, she scooted away from the deadly thing.

14:25 and counting. And Eddie sat between her and the metal door he'd pulled shut behind them. Had he found another way to lock it? She was surrounded by solid walls and a room full of potential shrapnel. This bomb wasn't about bringing down the school or hurting anyone else. This was all about her. Daisy thought she might be sick. It had always been about destroying her.

She flinched when she felt his hand on her hair. "Why don't you say Merry Christmas to me? I've seen your room and your house. I know how you love the holidays. You're the only gift I want. I love you."

Ignoring the swimming focus of her vision, she stood. "We need to get out of here."

"We're exactly where we need to be. Together." His tone was so patient, so sweet, so creepy.

"How long was I out?"

"A few minutes. Long enough for me to make sure we won't be bothered in these final, precious moments."

"Final?"

He stood and came toward her. "It's the only way we can be together."

She backed away from his outstretched hand until she ran into a rack of chairs. Everything around her rattled, giving her an idea. A heavy metal chair could be as effective as a baseball bat if she could get her hands on one. The knot on her head and the wound on Albert's scalp told her Eddie had probably already thought of that.

Albert. "Eddie, there's a student on the other side of that wall. You don't want to hurt him."

"I've done my calculations. Albert finally served a meaningful purpose." Bait to lure her down here was hardly something to brag about. "He and Bernie were wastes of time and space in your life."

"Bernie? You hurt him, too?"

Eddie touched the front of his coat. "Once I borrowed his jacket again, I didn't need him anymore."

"It was you the night of the fire."

"I was afraid your soldier boy saw me."

"He did. But he couldn't identify you. We suspected Coach Riley. His jacket…" she inhaled a sniff of the stale air around her "…*that* jacket smelled like smoke."

"Do you honestly think that blockhead knows anything other than sports?" Eddie snickered as he rested his hand on the rack beside her head and leaned in. "I've borrowed his hat and coat a couple of times since his wife kicked him out and he's been keeping an extra set of clothes at school. It's a smart way to divert suspicion off me, don't you think?"

Yeah, Eddie was smart. Crazy. But smart. She eyed the tubes of chemicals on the floor behind him. "Now you've built a bomb. Is there more than one?"

He grabbed her chin and forced her gaze back to his. "We just need the one."

She nearly gagged at the taste of his mouth sliding over hers. Although she suspected she needed to stay calm and try to talk her way out of this, she couldn't squash down her fight-or-flight response. She shoved him away, slipped to one side, grabbing a chair off the rack. Several more chairs crashed to the floor, forcing him another step back, giving her a chance to swing the chair in her hands. The blow caught him in the shoulder, knocking him to his knees.

Daisy scrambled toward the door. But the very chairs that had created a barrier between them now became a blockade she had to push aside and climb over. Before she could touch the metal latch, Eddie's arms closed around her from behind, lifting her off her feet before he slammed her into the wall beside the door. She screamed at the pain of her head knocking into another hard object. Her glasses got knocked sideways. But she pushed back. "Let go of me!"

Eddie threw his whole body against hers, crushing her against the wall. He spat against her ear. "You held me the night I told you about Jenny—how she left me."

"Your fiancée died." It was hard to talk with her face mashed against the wall.

But Eddie wasn't listening. "I was there for you after that Brock fiasco, I was at your father's funeral, holding your hand. We have a connection you can't deny."

"We were friends."

"I love you."

"I don't love you."

"Liar!" He whipped her around, roughly clasping his face between her hands. She obliquely wondered what had happened to the cell phone and if losing track of it meant the bomb was going to go off any sooner. But she had a more immediate problem with the hands sliding down around her throat and the crazed anger in Eddie's eyes. "You confided in me. It was only a matter of time before you turned to me for something more. I encouraged Angelo's little crush on you because I knew it would bother you and you'd come looking for a man. For me. But then Soldier Boy came to town."

"Ed…die," she gasped.

His hands tightened around her throat. She didn't think he was strangling her on purpose, but he was so angry. He was beyond listening to reason. He was impervious to the scratch of her fingernails on his hands, begging him to free her. "Suddenly he's doing everything for you I'm supposed to. I was outside your house last night. I saw you go up to his room. You slept with him, didn't you?" She didn't answer. She couldn't. Incensed, he threw her away from him. "I knew it. You're a traitor. But I forgive you."

For once, she relished the cold, hard concrete because it meant she was free. For the moment. Daisy coughed her bruised airways clear and scooted away from Eddie's advance. "How did I betray you? I've always loved you as a friend."

"But you're *in* love with him, aren't you?"

"Yes." Even if no one else ever heard it, she was going to state the truth. "I love Harry Lockhart."

"I've shown you real love."

Her fingers brushed against the bomb and she screeched and rolled away. "Do you think I want a man to treat me like all those pictures? They scared me to death."

"They're love scenes."

"That isn't love. That's…a sickness." The pile of fallen chairs blocked her escape.

The anger left his tone, but the crazy remained. "That's how I think about you—about us—every night. I've loved you from that first night we were together."

"Drinking coffee," she reminded him, scrabbling to get to her feet. "Having a conversation. We have never been *together*."

"Stop fighting me on this. We are meant to be together. Always." He glanced away to look at the numbers ticking away on the bomb. "In another eleven minutes, we will be."

She had eleven minutes left to live? She'd fought off Brock and his knife, how did she fight a bomb? "How does the bomb work? When it reaches zero, it'll explode?"

"A small charge will blow out the stopper between the tubes. Then the chemicals will mix. Very volatile." He pulled her phone from the pocket of the jacket. "Or I can dial the number and detonate it sooner. Would you like that? It will be quick and painless, I promise."

"You've blown people up before?"

He smiled. "Such a wonderful sense of humor."

"I don't feel like laughing. Please, Eddie. Let me go. Let me get you some help."

"You're not leaving me."

Daisy dreamed she heard scratching outside the door. Fate coming to get her this time, she supposed. "What if I promise to come back? After you shut off the bomb and I know everyone is safe, you and I will sit down and talk."

"Liar! You'll go back to him." He reached for her again. "You're mine!"

The door behind Eddie slid open with a mighty shove. "Caliban, *Fass*!"

Attack.

A blur of black and tan charged into the room and lunged at Eddie's outstretched hand. Caliban clamped down on Eddie's forearm and knocked him to the floor. His fist hit the concrete and the cell phone skittered out of his grip. Eddie screamed. "No!"

Barely a step behind the attacking dog, Harry filled up the doorway, following the aim of the gun he held between his hands. "Down on the ground! Hands where I can see them!"

There was no time to feel relief or love or even fear of the one-man attack force looming over Eddie and taking charge of the room.

"Get the phone!" Her cell skittered away beneath a rack of chairs as Eddie and the dog struggled. She dove for the floor and stuck her arm beneath the rack, groping for the phone. "Don't let him push any numbers!"

"Damn it, Daisy. Stay back!"

"He can set off the bomb if he calls the number."

Eddie shrieked at the fangs sinking into his forearm and shaking him. "She's mine. You can't have her. She loves me."

Her fingers closed around the phone. "I've got it."

"Get behind me!" Harry ordered, moving between her and the dog and man wrestling and growling and screaming on the floor. "I'm going to call off the dog and you stay down. Understand? Do you understand?"

"Yes. Call him off."

"Caliban, *Hier*!"

The three-legged dog released Eddie and trotted back to Harry's side. Bloodied and dazed, Eddie reached into his pocket and pulled out his own cell phone. "She's mine!"

Harry knocked that phone to the concrete, crushed it beneath his boot. He smashed the butt of his gun across Eddie's face and knocked him out.

His big chest heaved with deep breaths as he grabbed her arm and pulled her close. His eyes were focused squarely on the bomb. "Are you hurt?"

"Not much."

"Stay behind me. I want my armor between us and that explosive in case it goes off early. We're backing out of this room." Daisy willingly latched on to the back of his vest and moved away from Eddie and the bomb. Part of her wanted to ask Harry why he was here. How had he known she needed him? How had he found her? Was he okay? Was this whole scene triggering the worst of his nightmares again? But she didn't ask any of those questions. The aim of his gun at the man on the floor never wavered.

"Caliban!" As the dog loped out into the hallway with them, Harry turned his mouth to the radio on the front of his vest. "This is Lockhart. Hostages are secure. Move in! Move in!"

"Albert!" Daisy hurried over to the young man who was sitting on the bottom step and hugged him in her arms. "Are you all right? I was so worried."

Harry was still talking into his radio, giving information. She heard an invasion of footfalls in the lobby above her, and suddenly two men in full battle gear were charging down the stairs. Another man and woman with rifles and SWAT armor came down the stairs at the opposite end of the hallway, converging on Harry's position.

"You've got just under eight minutes." Only when the four uniformed officers entered the storage room did Harry move. He holstered his gun and cupped her elbow, urging her onto her feet. "We gotta go, honey. Clock's ticking." He pulled Albert to his feet and bent to lift the young man over his shoulders in a fireman's carry. "Up the stairs and out the front door. Don't stop moving 'til I tell you."

She nodded and climbed the stairs, with Harry and Caliban following close on her heels. When they reached the lobby, she saw another officer helping Coach Riley out the door. There was blood matted in Bernie's hair. Apparently, Eddie had knocked him out, too. He'd probably been faking the radio conversation with Bernie that she'd overheard. "Is he okay?"

She felt Harry's hand at the small of her back.

"Keep movin', honey. There's still a bomb and we aren't safe. Take a right."

As soon as she hit the cold air outside the door, another officer ran forward to guide her through a line of armed responders and emergency vehicles toward the group of ambulances that were waiting in the parking lot. Even carrying Albert on his shoulders, Harry stayed close enough that she could feel him blocking the winter wind at her back.

A few minutes later, she was sitting in the back of an ambulance again while an EMT checked her vitals and crushed up an ice pack for her to hold against the knot on her head. She gasped when the back doors opened. Harry. Before she could say anything, he patted the floor of the ambulance. *"Hopp!"*

Her startled frown turned into a delighted smile when Caliban jumped up into the ambulance.

"Sir, you can't—"

"Come here, good boy." Daisy dropped the ice pack and welcomed her three-legged dog onto the gurney beside her, scratching all around his ears and kissing the top of his head as he rested his graying muzzle on her thigh. "I'm so glad you were there for Mama today. What a good, good boy." Because of this dog, she was alive. She tilted her aching head up to Harry. Because of this man, she was alive. "Is it over?"

His gray eyes reflected the bright morning light. "All except for the cleanup. The bomb was easy to defuse. A matter of disconnecting wires." His battle-scarred face was lined with concern as he studied her. "A hazmat unit is going in now to deal with the chemicals. KCPD has taken Bosch into custody."

Tears stung the corners of her eyes. She hadn't cried once when Eddie had touched her, hurt her, threatened her life. But she was about to bawl just looking at the man she loved so much.

"Give us a minute, will you?" Harry asked.

The EMT nodded and climbed out of the ambulance as Harry climbed in.

Harry picked up the fallen ice pack and sat on the other side of Caliban, reaching over the dog to hold the pack in place at the crown of her head. "Are you really in one piece?"

"Nothing a hot shower won't cure." She slipped her hand over Caliban's back to grasp Harry's thigh. "Thank you. Eddie was…" She couldn't fathom how skewed that man's brain must be to think that he loved her and that killing her was his idea of the two of them being committed to each other. A hot tear spilled over and trailed down her cheek. "I really attract the crazies, don't I?"

Harry wiped the tear away with the pad of his thumb. "I'm not going to be one of them."

A tiny knife of guilt stabbed her in the heart. She reached up to cup the side of his jaw. "I didn't mean you."

"But you're worried that me suiting up and coming after you may have triggered another episode. It didn't."

"Are you really okay?"

He shrugged and her hand dropped away. "Okay enough."

"What does that mean?" She turned to face him. "Harry, you have to know that I have feelings for you. As relieved as I was to see you coming through that door, I would never want to do anything to set back your recovery."

"You didn't do a damn thing. Bosch and no one else is responsible for what happened to you and Albert and Coach Riley today."

"Albert!" She pushed Caliban's head off her leg and tried to stand. "I need to find out if he's okay."

Harry caught her as she tripped over his feet, and pulled her down onto his lap. "He's fine. A concussion and some stitches. He and Coach Riley are in another ambulance, getting treatment. Angelo is with him and their grandmother is on her way. Right now, the only person you have to save is you."

"But if I can help…"

Harry feathered his fingers into her hair and straightened her bent glasses. "Damn it, woman, if you won't think about yourself, then think about me. I just saved your life. And I didn't crack up doing it. You're safe. It's over. And I love you." His stiff, handsome mouth crooked into a smile. "Don't you want to hug me?"

Daisy threw her arms around his neck as he pulled her to his chest. His hands fisted in the back of her coat and his nose nestled into the hair at her temple. She held on tight with all the love in her heart and wept happy tears.

Epilogue

After the last of the guests had left the party and the dogs had curled up on the couch, Harry reached beneath the Christmas tree and pulled out the present he'd wrapped for Daisy. The narrow, rectangular shape told her it couldn't be anything other than his journal. "I want you to know exactly who this is from."

Tears stung her eyes as he pulled her into his lap on the recliner. "Are you sure you want me to read this?"

"I wouldn't share it with anybody else." His arms settled around her waist and she detected a faint trembling in them. "I do a lot better telling you what I feel when I write it down." He took the ribbon and paper from her and tossed them aside. His chest expanded with a deep, steadying breath, and she knew that Harry was the bravest man she'd ever known. "Start at the end."

She pressed a kiss to his mouth, thanking him for entrusting her with this gift before turning her attention to the spiral notebook, thumbing through the pages until she reached the last entry.

Dear Daisy,

I never thought I could be anything but a marine. Nothing useful, anyway. The Corps gave me purpose and a home when I desperately needed those things. I love my job more than anything I've ever done. If they'll still have me—if I pass the psych tests—I want to go on being a marine until I'm ready to retire in another two years.

These ten days I've spent with you, though, got me thinking about other things. I came to you with the idea that the Daisy from your letters could save me—that you were this magic angel who could reach inside my head, erase the nightmares and make me whole again. Turns out you weren't anything like that angel. You're bold and brave. You touch and you talk. You weren't as much of a lady as I thought you'd be, and you frustrated the hell out of me more than once. There wasn't any mystical glow about you. But you ~~were~~ are real. You're heart and color and acceptance and hope and life and love. I'm a better man for knowing you and being a part of your crazy life. I'm healthier. Happier. I'm home when I'm with you. You weren't the woman I imagined, but you turned out to be exactly the woman I needed.

I've got some ideas now on what I could do

*when I leave the Corps, whether it's in a month
or two years. Training dogs. Working as a cop
or search and rescue with the fire department.
Maybe you can even help me get through college so I can be a teacher or social worker who
works with kids like Albert and 'Lo.*

*One thing I'm certain of, now and forever, is
that I love you. If you can put up with a marine
who's gone on and off for a couple of years,
or with a washed-up master sergeant who isn't
sure what he's going to do with the rest of his
life, I want to marry you. I hope I can get my
act together well enough that you would consider saying yes.*

Love,
Harry

Daisy's heart swelled up and spilled over in a sob
of hot, flowing tears. She threw her arms around his
neck and hugged him tight.

His hands fisted in the back of her sweater, holding on to her just as tightly. "Is there anything I can
write that won't make you cry?"

"A grocery list?"

He laughed, and she scrambled off his lap and ran
to the kitchen, pulling a red pen from her purse. Harry
followed her, winding his arms around her waist and
resting his chin on her shoulder while she scrawled a
message at the end of the letter. "You're going English teacher on me now? Checking my grammar?"

She signed the short missive and held it up to show it to him. "Here's my letter to you."

Dear Harry,
I love you. With all my heart. I know we can
get through anything together.
   When you ask, my answer is YES!
Love,
Daisy

* * * * *

Look for more books from USA TODAY
bestselling author Julie Miller in 2018.

And don't miss the titles in her recent miniseries,
THE PRECINCT: BACHELORS IN BLUE:

APB: BABY
KANSAS CITY COUNTDOWN
NECESSARY ACTION
PROTECTION DETAIL

Available now from Harlequin Intrigue!

Sheriff Flint Cahill can and will endure elements far worse than the coming winter storm to hunt down Maggie Thompson and her abductor.

Read on for a sneak preview of
COWBOY'S LEGACY,
A CAHILL RANCH NOVEL *from*
New York Times bestselling author
B.J. Daniels!

SHE WAS IN so fast that she didn't have a chance to scream. The icy cold water stole her breath away. Her eyes flew open as she hit. Because of the way she fell, she had no sense of up or down for a few moments.

Panicked, she flailed in the water until a light flickered above her. She tried to swim toward it, but something was holding her down. The harder she fought, the more it seemed to push her deeper and deeper, the light fading.

Her lungs burned. She had to breathe. The dim light wavered above her through the rippling water. She clawed at it as her breath gave out. She could see the surface just inches above her. Air! She needed oxygen. Now!

The rippling water distorted the face that suddenly appeared above her. The mouth twisted in a grotesque smile. She screamed, only to have her throat fill with the putrid dark water. She choked, sucking in even more water. She was drowning, and the person who'd done this to her was watching her die and smiling.

Maggie Thompson shot upright in bed, gasping for air and swinging her arms frantically toward the faint light coming through the window. Panic had her perspiration-soaked nightgown sticking to her skin. Trembling, she clutched the bedcovers as she gasped for breath.

The nightmare had been so real this time that she thought she was going to drown before she could come out of it. Her chest ached, her throat feeling raw as tears burned her eyes. It had been too real. She couldn't shake the feeling that she'd almost died this time. Next time…

She snapped on the bedside lamp to chase away the dark shadows hunkered in the corners of the room. If only Flint had been here instead of on an all-night stakeout. She needed Sheriff Flint Cahill's strong arms around her. Not that he stayed most nights. They hadn't been intimate that long.

Often, he had to work or was called out in the middle of the night. He'd asked her to move in with him months ago, but she'd declined. He'd asked her after one of his ex-wife's nasty tricks. Maggie hadn't wanted to make a decision like that based on Flint's ex.

While his ex hadn't done anything in months to keep them apart, Maggie couldn't rest easy. Flint was hoping Celeste had grown tired of her tricks. Maggie wasn't that naive. Celeste Duma was one of those women who played on every man's weakness to get what she wanted—and she wanted not just the rich, powerful man she'd left Flint for. She wanted to keep her ex on the string, as well.

Maggie's breathing slowed a little. She pulled the covers up to her chin, still shivering, but she didn't turn off the light. Sleep was out of the question for a while. She told herself that she wasn't going to let Celeste scare her. She wasn't going to give the woman the satisfaction.

Unfortunately, it was just bravado. Flint's ex was obsessed with him. Obsessed with keeping them apart. And since the woman had nothing else to do…

As the images of the nightmare faded, she reminded herself that the dream made no sense. It never had. She was a good swimmer. Loved water. Had never nearly drowned. Nor had anyone ever tried to drown her.

Shuddering, she thought of the face she'd seen through the rippling water. Not Celeste's. More like a Halloween mask. A distorted smiling face, neither male nor female. Just the memory sent her heart racing again.

What bothered her most was that dream kept reoccurring. After the first time, she'd mentioned it to her friend, Belle Delaney.

"A drowning dream?" Belle had asked with the arch of her eyebrow. "Do you feel that in waking life you're being 'sucked into' something you'd rather not be a part of?"

Maggie had groaned inwardly. Belle had never kept it a secret that she thought Maggie was making a mistake when it came to Flint. Too much baggage, she always said of the sheriff. His "baggage" came in the shape of his spoiled, probably psychopathic, petite, green-eyed, blonde ex.

"I have my own skeletons." Maggie had laughed, although she'd never shared her past—even with Belle—before moving to Gilt Edge, Montana, and opening her beauty shop, Just Hair. She feared it was her own baggage that scared her the most.

"If you're holding anything back," Belle had said, eyeing her closely, "you need to let it out. Men hate surprises after they tie the knot."

"Guess I don't have to worry about that because Flint hasn't said anything about marriage." But she knew Belle was right. She'd even come close to telling him several times about her past. Something had always stopped her. The truth was, she feared if he found out her reasons for coming to Gilt Edge he wouldn't want her anymore.

"The dream isn't about Flint," she'd argued that day with Belle, but she couldn't shake the feeling that it was a warning.

"Well, from what I know about dreams," Belle had said, "if in the dream you survive the drowning, it means that a waking relationship will ultimately survive the turmoil. At least, that is one interpretation. But I'd say the nightmare definitely indicates that you are going into unknown waters and something is making you leery of where you're headed." She'd cocked an eyebrow at her. "If you have the dream again, I'd suggest that you ask yourself what it is you're so afraid of."

"I'm sure it's just about his ex, Celeste," she'd lied. Or was she afraid that she wasn't good enough for Flint—just as his ex had warned her. Just as she feared in her heart.

THE WIND LAY over the tall dried grass and kicked up dust as Sheriff Flint Cahill stood on the hillside. He shoved his Stetson down on his head of thick dark hair, squinting in the distance at the clouds to the west. Sure as the devil, it was going to snow before the day was out.

In the distance, he could see a large star made out of red and green lights on the side of a barn, a reminder that Christmas was coming. Flint thought he might even get a tree this year, go up in the mountains and cut it himself. He hadn't had a tree at Christmas in years. Not since…

At the sound of a pickup horn, he turned, shielding his eyes from the low winter sun. He could smell snow in the air, feel it deep in his bones. This storm was going to dump a good foot on them, according to the latest news. They were going to have a white Christmas.

Most years he wasn't ready for the holiday season any more than he was ready for a snow that wouldn't melt until spring. But this year was different. He felt energized. This was the year his life would change. He thought of the small velvet box in his jacket pocket. He'd been carrying it around for months. Just the thought of it made him smile to himself. He was in love and he was finally going to do something about it.

The pickup rumbled to a stop a few yards from him. He took a deep breath of the mountain air and, telling himself he was ready for whatever Mother Nature wanted to throw at him, he headed for the truck.

"Are you all right?" his sister asked as he slid into the passenger seat. In the cab out of the wind, it was nice and warm. He rubbed his bare hands together, wishing he hadn't forgotten his gloves earlier. But when he'd headed out, he'd had too much on his mind. He still did.

Lillie looked out at the dull brown of the landscape and the chain-link fence that surrounded the missile silo. "What were you doing out here?"

He chuckled. "Looking for aliens. What else?" This was the spot that their father swore aliens hadn't just landed on one night back in 1967. Nope, according to Ely Cahill, the aliens had abducted him, taken him aboard their spaceship and done experiments on him. Not that anyone believed it in the county. Everyone just assumed that Ely had a screw loose. Or two.

It didn't help that their father spent most of the year up in the mountains as a recluse trapping and panning for gold.

"Aliens. Funny," Lillie said, making a face at him.

He smiled over at her. "Actually, I was on an all-night stakeout. The cattle rustlers didn't show up." He shrugged.

She glanced around. "Where's your patrol SUV?"

"Axle deep in a muddy creek back toward Grass Range. I'll have to get it pulled out. After I called you, I started walking and I ended up here. Wish I'd grabbed my gloves, though."

"You're scaring me," she said, studying him openly. "You're starting to act like Dad."

He laughed at that, wondering how far from the truth it was. "At least I didn't see any aliens near the missile silo."

She groaned. Being the butt of jokes in the county because of their father got old for all of them.

Flint glanced at the fenced-in area. There was nothing visible behind the chain link but tumbleweeds. He turned back to her. "I didn't pull you away from anything important, I hope? Since you were close by, I thought you wouldn't mind giving me a ride. I've had enough walking for one day. Or thinking, for that matter."

She shook her head. "What's going on, Flint?"

He looked out at the country that ran to the mountains. Cahill Ranch. His grandfather had started it, his father had worked it and now two of his brothers ran the cattle part of it to keep the place going while he and his sister, Lillie, and brother Darby had taken other paths. Not to mention their oldest brother, Tucker, who'd struck out at seventeen and hadn't been seen or heard from since.

Flint had been scared after his marriage and divorce. But Maggie was nothing like Celeste, who was small, blonde, green-eyed and crazy. Maggie was tall with big brown eyes and long auburn hair. His heart beat faster at the thought of her smile, at her laugh.

"I'm going to ask Maggie to marry me," Flint said and nodded as if reassuring himself.

When Lillie didn't reply, he glanced over at her. It wasn't like her not to have something to say. "Well?"

"What has taken you so long?"

He sighed. "Well, you know after Celeste…"

"Say no more," his sister said, raising a hand to stop him. "Anyone would be gun-shy after being married to her."

"I'm hoping she won't be a problem."

Lillie laughed. "Short of killing your ex-wife, she is always going to be a problem. You just have to decide if you're going to let her run your life. Or if you're going to live it—in spite of her."

So easy for her to say. He smiled, though. "You're right. Anyway, Maggie and I have been dating for a while now and there haven't been any…incidents in months."

Lillie shook her head. "You know Celeste was the one who vandalized Maggie's beauty shop—just as you know she started that fire at Maggie's house."

"Too bad there wasn't any proof so I could have arrested her. But since there wasn't and no one was hurt and it was months ago…"

"I'd love to see Celeste behind bars, though I think prison is too good for her. I can understand why you would be worried about what she will do next. She's psychopathic."

He feared that that maybe was close to the case.

"Do you want to see the ring?" He knew she did, so he fished it out of his pocket. He'd been carrying it around for quite a while now. Getting up his courage? He knew what was holding him back. Celeste. He couldn't be sure how she would take it—or what she might do. His ex-wife seemed determined that he and Maggie shouldn't be together, even though she was apparently happily married to local wealthy businessman Wayne Duma.

Handing his sister the small black velvet box, he waited as she slowly opened it.

A small gasp escaped her lips. "It's beautiful. *Really* beautiful." She shot him a look. "I thought sheriffs didn't make much money?"

"I've been saving for a long while now. Unlike my sister, I live pretty simply."

She laughed. "Simply? Prisoners have more in their cells than you do. You aren't thinking of living in that small house of yours after you're married, are you?"

"For a while. It's not that bad. Not all of us have huge new houses like you and Trask."

"We need the room for all the kids we're going to have," she said. "But it is wonderful, isn't it? Trask is determined that I have everything I ever wanted." Her gaze softened as the newlywed thought of her husband.

"I keep thinking of your wedding." There'd been a double wedding, with both Lillie and her twin, Darby, getting married to the loves of their lives only months ago. "It's great to see you and Trask so happy.

And Darby and Mariah… I don't think Darby is ever going to come off that cloud he's on."

Lillie smiled. "I'm so happy for him. And I'm happy for you. You know I really like Maggie. So do it. Don't worry about Celeste. Once you're married, there's nothing she can do."

He told himself she was right, and yet in the back of his mind, he feared that his ex-wife would do something to ruin it—just as she had done to some of his dates with Maggie.

"I don't understand Celeste," Lillie was saying as she shifted into Drive and started toward the small Western town of Gilt Edge. "She's the one who dumped you for Wayne Duma. So what is her problem?"

"I'm worried that she is having second thoughts about her marriage to Duma. Or maybe she's bored and has nothing better to do than concern herself with my life. Maybe she just doesn't want me to be happy."

"Or she is just plain malicious," Lillie said. "If she isn't happy, she doesn't want you to be, either."

A shaft of sunlight came through the cab window, warming him against the chill that came with even talking about Celeste. He leaned back, content as Lillie drove.

He was going to ask Maggie to marry him. He was going to do it this weekend. He'd already made a dinner reservation at the local steak house. He had the ring in his pocket. Now it was just a matter of popping the question and hoping she said yes. If she did… Well, then, this was going to be the best Christmas ever, he thought and smiled.

* * * * *

Don't miss COWBOY'S LEGACY,
available December 2017
wherever HQN Books and
ebooks are sold.

www.Harlequin.com

COMING NEXT MONTH FROM
ⓗ HARLEQUIN®

INTRIGUE

Available December 19, 2017

#1755 GUNFIRE ON THE RANCH
Blue River Ranch • by Delores Fossen
DEA agent Theo Carter was a suspect in his parents' murder...and now he's back to protect the family he never knew he had.

#1756 SAFE AT HAWK'S LANDING
Badge of Justice • by Rita Herron
Charlotte Reacher is no stranger to the trauma her students have experienced, and as she's the only witness to a human-trafficking abduction, FBI agent Lucas Hawk will have his work cut out for him keeping her safe.

#1757 WHISPERING SPRINGS
by Amanda Stevens
This high school reunion was a shot at redemption and maybe a second chance for former army ranger Dylan Burkhart and his old flame Ava North. But a secret-telling game turns up a murder confession, with the killer hiding among them...

#1758 RANGER PROTECTOR
Texas Brothers of Company B • by Angi Morgan
After Megan Harper is framed for a fatal shooting, protecting her becomes Texas Ranger Jack McKinnon's sole mission...until unspoken desire gets in the way.

#1759 SOLDIER'S PROMISE
The Ranger Brigade: Family Secrets • by Cindi Myers
Different circumstances brought officer Jake Lohmiller and undercover Ranger Brigade sergeant Carmen Redhorse to a cult encampment in Colorado, but teaming up might be their only shot at saving their families... and each other.

#1760 FORGOTTEN PIECES
The Protectors of Riker County • by Tyler Anne Snell
To say Riker County detective Matt Walker and journalist Maggie Carson have bad blood is an understatement. But when the last twenty-four hours of her memory go missing and she gets caught in someone's crosshairs, the lawman who hates her may be her only salvation...

YOU CAN FIND MORE INFORMATION ON UPCOMING HARLEQUIN® TITLES, FREE EXCERPTS AND MORE AT WWW.HARLEQUIN.COM.

HICNM1217

Get 2 Free Books,

Plus 2 Free Gifts—

just for trying the Reader Service!

Everyone worked through grief differently.

Some people started a new hobby; some people threw themselves into the gym.

Others investigated unsolved murders in secret.

"And why, of all people, would you need me here?" Matt asked, cutting through her mental breakdown of him.

Instead of stepping backward, utilizing the large open space of her front porch, she chanced a step forward.

"I found something," she started, straining out any excess enthusiasm that might make her seem coarse. Still, she knew the detective was a keen observer. Which was why his frown was already doubling in on itself before she explained herself.

"I don't want to hear this," he interrupted, his voice like ice. "I'm warning you, Carson."

"And it wouldn't be the first time you've done so," she countered, skipping over the fact he'd said her last name like a teacher getting ready to send her to detention. "But right now I'm telling you I found a lead. A real, honest-to-God lead!"

The detective's frown affected all of his body. It pinched his expression and pulled his posture taut. Through gritted teeth, he rumbled out his thoughts with disdain clear in his words.

"Why do you keep doing this? What gives you the right?" He took a step away from her. That didn't stop Maggie.

"It wasn't an accident," she implored. "I can prove it now."

Matt shook his head. He skipped frustrated and flew right into angry. This time Maggie faltered.

"You have no right digging into this," he growled. "You didn't even know Erin."

"But don't you want to hear what I found?"

Matt made a stop motion with his hands. The jaw she'd been admiring was set. Hard. "I don't want to ever talk to you again. Especially about this." He turned and was off the front porch in one fluid motion. Before he got into his truck he paused. "And next time you call me out here, I won't hesitate to arrest you."

And then he was gone.

Don't miss
FORGOTTEN PIECES
available January 2018 wherever
Harlequin® Intrigue books and ebooks are sold.

www.Harlequin.com

THE WORLD IS BETTER WITH

Romance

Harlequin has everything from contemporary, passionate and heartwarming to suspenseful and inspirational stories.

Whatever your mood,
we have a romance just for you!

Connect with us to find your next great read,
special offers and more.

f /HarlequinBooks

🐦 @HarlequinBooks

www.HarlequinBlog.com

www.Harlequin.com/Newsletters

HARLEQUIN

A *Romance* FOR EVERY MOOD™

www.Harlequin.com